D1089693

THE SUM...
FELL IN LOVE

Saint turned the corner and headed for Tina's. This meant only one thing: he was going to drop me off last.

Tina smiled and waved to us as we left her on the curb. I swear I saw her wink at me when we drove off.

"Jen, how about checking out the new movie that's coming next week?" the dreamy voice said, as we pulled up in front of my house.

He turned to face me again. Me. Jenny Ryan.

"I'll pick you up next Saturday night at eight-thirty, OK?"

"OK," I breathed, as I got out of the car and floated up the walk. Suddenly a shadow moved behind me and I came down to earth in a hurry.

It was Cliff. . . .

Bantam Sweet Dreams Romances
Ask your bookseller for the books you have missed

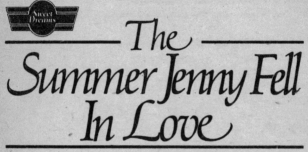

The Summer Jenny Fell In Love

Barbara Conklin

BANTAM BOOKS
TORONTO · NEW YORK · LONDON · SYDNEY

RL 6, IL age 11 and up

THE SUMMER JENNY FELL IN LOVE
A Bantam Book / July 1982

Cover photo by Pat Hill

Sweet Dreams and its associated logo are trademarks of
Bantam Books, Inc.

All rights reserved.
Copyright © 1982 by Barbara Conklin and Cloverdale Press.

*This book may not be reproduced in whole or in part, by
mineograph or any other means, without permission. For
information address: Bantam Books, Inc.*

ISBN 0-553-20789-X

Published simultaneously in the United States and Canada

*Bantam Books are published by Bantam Books, Inc. Its trademark,
consisting of the words "Bantam Books" and the portrayal of a
rooster, is Registered in U.S. Patent and Trademark Office and in
other countries. Marca Registrada. Bantam Books, Inc., 666 Fifth
Avenue, New York, New York 10103.*

PRINTED IN THE UNITED STATES OF AMERICA

0 9 8 7 6 5 4

To my father and mother,
Carl and Prudence Seyfried.
If they could see me now—
they would be so proud.

Foreword

Today I start cleaning out my closets and drawers in my bedroom. It isn't by choice. My mother has given the order through the chain of command (my grandmother) and as usual, I have put it off as long as possible.

My mother puts two huge boxes in my room with the directions to place all of my junk in them. I can't imagine why she thinks I keep junk in this room. Everything I have has a sentimental value, and that's why it is so hard to get rid of anything.

Lying in the middle of my bed is a small blue jar of lipstick—my original shade. You can't find it in the stores anywhere. A tiny ring box is right next to that. Inside on a square of cotton rests an artificial nail, the dried glue still on its underside.

There is a rolled-up pencil sketch of my grandmother. The artist had thrown it away in disgust, but I dug it out of the trash because I thought it was fantastic. Next to that are four typed pages on my future career, and next to that a business card on which three little mermaids with brooms are dancing. Over their heads are the words, The Sand Sweepers. The real Sand Sweepers are in a photo right next to that.

Joann is the tall blond on the far left. The girl on the right, the short one with all that chestnut, billowy hair, is Tina. I'm in the middle, and in this picture you can hardly see my freckles. The ocean air got to my hair that day, though, and the light brown waves just swept all over the place.

All of these items will fit neatly in a shoe box and will take up very little room on the top of my closet shelf. I'll have to label the contents, though, so that in years to come, when I open it, I will remember what all of these things meant to me.

I laugh at that. How could I ever forget the pain, the joy, the sadness, the happiness these little things brought to me?

I pick up the black marking pen and start to print in large bold letters: THE SUMMER JENNY FELL IN LOVE.

Chapter 1

It was June 8, only two days after school had closed, when my mother dropped the bomb—right at the kitchen table.

"There's this woman I work with," she said, brushing her red hair out of her eyes with her fingers. "Her name is Ellen Morrow. She's having a rough time of it. Moneywise, that is."

"Poor soul," my grandmother said, half-listening, reading the morning paper.

"Ellen moved here with her son Cliff from Philadelphia a little less than two months ago," my mother went on, delicately dabbing her lipstick with a paper napkin. She's been divorced for two years, and had been struggling to make a living in Philadelphia. Then through a friend, she heard of this opportunity in our office for another good legal secretary. But in the time she's been here, she still hasn't found a decent place to live."

"Why?" Grandma asked, neatly folding the

paper and placing it alongside her shredded wheat with strawberries. "Apartments—nice ones—are being built everywhere. Why, they're tearing up all the orange groves, lima bean and strawberry fields—"

"I mean, one she can afford," my mother explained.

"But if it's a good job, Trish," my grandmother protested.

"You know, Mother, rents are sky-high and going higher," my mother answered, "and Ellen is saving for her son's education. She just lives for that boy, I'm afraid. He's the only thing in her life now, and she wants to make sure he has a good chance. At least here in California the colleges' tuitions are reasonable. That's another reason why she chose to move here."

I was just taking a big bite out of a gooey pineapple Danish when she finally came right out and said it.

"I've asked her to move in with us," she told Grandma. "We could use the extra income. Since you've turned the sewing room into your room, we've got your old bedroom upstairs. Mrs. Morrow can take that room," my mother went on, sipping her coffee, "and her son can sleep in the room over the garage. It's only a junk and catchall room anyhow."

I nearly choked. "A junk room! A catchall!" I cried out, dribbling crumbs down my T-shirt. "What are you saying!"

I'm as tall as my mother, and our eyes come pretty even when we're both sitting down at the table, but now she seemed to be looking down at me from a high stool.

"You're acting like a child," she said, and her green-blue eyes turned dark.

"She is a child," Grandma said, smiling at me.

"I'm not a child!" I protested. "I'll be seventeen in November. Grandma, you got married when you were seventeen, and you had your first baby when you were only eighteen!"

My grandmother smiled again and picked up her paper, holding it in front of her as though to cut off any conversation about her early years. My mother immediately took up the slack.

"Jenny, we've got to be practical. Since you were three and your father died, I've been hard put to make ends meet."

"But I need that room," I went on, trying to remember all the hard times we'd been through. "I do most of my experimenting in there. And the light is better, and I can think better in there."

"Then do you want that room for yourself now?" Mom asked.

"No," I said quickly, unwilling to give up the space in my bedroom either. "But that room is my work place."

I could remember when Grandpa had built it. It was just after we moved in, when I was about eight. He and Grandma had finally persuaded my mother to give up her little house in Saginaw, Michigan, and move here to Sandcastle. My grandparents put a small down payment on this house, and my mother helped with the mortgage payments so we could all live together. There was plenty of room for that. Downstairs there was a great, bright kitchen with two windows looking right out at the ocean. The dining room had the same view through a large window made up of tiny squares of glass that could be hinged outward. Then there was the cozy, always warm sun porch right off of the dining area. In the front of the house, facing the street, was a huge living room and a small sewing room, where my grandmother slept now, with a good-sized closet, which my grandfather had turned into a bathroom.

My mother took the front upstairs bedroom, the one that looked out over the street. I took one of the two back bedrooms, and at that time Grandma and Grandpa had the other.

Our garage was attached to the house and jutted out to the left of it. Grandpa took one look at it and announced his intentions of building a room, with a big picture window, over it which he would attach to the second story of the house.

And he did. He turned it into a place where he could sit and work at making his bookcases and bread boxes and where he could paint. He was forever working on landscapes. It was a very special room, and he let me visit him often.

He died when I was twelve, and eventually I turned the space into my workroom. How could Mom even *think* of asking me to give it up?

"I need *both* rooms," I told my mother. "I really need that big closet, but I have to have the other room, too, for all of my makeup bottles and books and my stereo—"

"I'll be late," my mother said, pushing herself away from the table, evading my protests. "It's already decided."

I looked over to my grandmother for assistance, but it was quite apparent she wasn't going to give me any. What a traitor, I thought. Getting me interested in my natural cosmetics and skin-care career and then dumping me when I needed her the most!

"You have two weeks to clean out that room," my mother said, in her "and-that-is-final" tone. She might as well have said, "Jenny Ryan, you have been evicted!"

Some of the crumbs still in my mouth crept down my throat and choked me. I grabbed my orange juice and helped them down.

"That's the pits!" I called after her as she disappeared into the downstairs bathroom. My grandmother shook her head because she hates that expression, but I only use it when I really mean it.

With perfectly manicured, light-pink fingernails, Grandma tore open a tiny package of Sweet 'n Low and dumped it on her shredded wheat. Daintily she reached over and picked up the carton of low-fat milk and poured a small amount over the strawberries.

"It's the wild mane of hair," she said, picking up her spoon. "I've always said it was the hair. You both have it—you and your mother.

Your grandfather had it too, and your temper seems to go right along with it."

"I'll change," I told her darkly. "If that's what it is, if that's what makes me feel so mean sometimes, I'll cut it."

"Nonsense," Grandma said. "Now, Jenny, what do you say we start right now? I'll help you clean out that room."

I got up, yawned, and brushed the crumbs from my jeans. "Sorry, Grandma. I've got to go to work. Remember?"

"Oh, that cleaning thing," my grandmother said. "What was it, something like sandpipers?"

"The Sand Sweepers," I told her. "Joann and Tina and I are going to work at those two motels, The Moonglow and Rest-Awhile. When the regular maids are too busy, we'll fill in and do jobs like window washing and waxing floors, the kinds of things maids don't have time to do."

She laughed. "That's right. Three little mermaids with brooms," she said, referring to the business cards Joann's father had made up for us.

"But it's serious," I protested.

"It always is, dear," my grandmother said. "But when you return today—"

"It won't be until after two."

"That's okay," she said. "I'll help you then." She put her arm around my shoulders. "Jenny, we've got to back your mother in this, and if we start out right today, she'll know we're behind her."

Quickly I pecked my grandmother's cheek.

"Okay, okay," I told her, but my heart wasn't in it.

I grabbed an elastic out of the miscellaneous drawer near the kitchen sink (we called it the mess drawer), and I pulled my hair, and wound the elastic around it. Maybe I *would* cut it, I thought as I ran out the back door heading for Tina's house.

Chapter 2

It usually takes exactly three minutes to run to Tina Morgan's house from mine, but that morning it took me two at the most. I'd promised the manager at the Rest-Awhile that my crew would arrive at nine o'clock every Monday morning all summer. But it was already eight-forty-five, and I was fifteen minutes off my schedule.

I banged on Tina's kitchen door and shook the sand out of my beach walkers. My heart fell at least two inches when, through the white lace curtain at the door's window, I saw Mrs. Morgan instead of Tina.

Quickly she unlocked the door, her bleached blond hair falling over her face.

"Oh, my God, it's that late already!" she exclaimed, trying to pull her blue flannel robe around her chest. Mrs. Morgan is a little heavy, and the robe must have been bought a long

10

time ago because it would take more than just a little pulling for it to cover her whole front.

"We don't have too much time," I told Mrs. Morgan. "I promised Mr. Bronstein we'd be there by nine at the latest!"

Just then, a sleepy-eyed Tina walked into the kitchen. "Oh, it's you," Tina said. "I heard the banging."

I don't think she was taking our job seriously.

"Of course it's me," I told her, annoyed. "Look, it's late. C'mon and get dressed."

Mrs. Morgan moaned and headed for her own bedroom. I couldn't blame her, for she worked the four to midnight shift at one of the local restaurants.

"Okay," Tina said, wiping the sleep out of her eyes. "But I've got to brush my teeth."

I followed her into the closet-sized bathroom and watched her fumble for the toothpaste. Tying a red scarf around her hair, she bent over the sink and splashed her flawless complexion with cold water. Then I watched her gently pat it dry with a huge yellow bath towel. Not a freckle, I thought. Not a single one.

She saw me staring. "Still waiting for me to get freckles?" she asked as she filled her toothbrush with toothpaste. She knew me too well.

With her free hand she pointed at my face, and I stood beside her looking into the bathroom mirror.

"There are still seven of them," I told her, glaring at my reddish-brown freckles.

"That's not bad," she said, trying to talk and rinse out her mouth at the same time. "Just six months ago you had twenty or so."

"Twenty-two," I told her. "Grandma's cream is pretty good, but still those last seven need something stronger."

I watched Tina brush her shoulder-length, chestnut brown hair.

"Are you sure I don't have time for a shower?" she pleaded again as we walked down the hall toward her room.

"Oh, Tina," I moaned. "Let's go!"

"Okay, okay," she said. I followed her into her bedroom. She struggled out of her green flannel nightgown, then gave a quick shake of her shoulders as the morning chill encircled her. Off a bedroom chair she grabbed a pair of cutoffs and a yellow T-shirt that stated: When you're tired of the rest—try the best. Then we were off.

Joann Casper was waiting for us right outside her apartment building. It is the only high-rise in Sandcastle, and it sits right on our same stretch of Sea Gull Drive, only four blocks down the street from Tina's.

"Well, at least you're ready," I told Joann, who had been leaning against the brick building. She was dressed in her cutoffs, too, and I wondered momentarily if I would be too hot in my jeans.

We crossed the dirt road and headed for the Rest-Awhile Motel. As the white stucco building came into view, we broke into a run. We were already late, and on our first day! When we were almost there, I decided to break the news to them, figuring another minute or two late wouldn't make a difference. The truth was, I simply couldn't hold it in any longer.

Trying to catch my breath, I said, "The most awful thing happened to me this morning."

They both slowed down, and I realized that I had their complete attention.

"My mother is renting part of our house out to a woman she works with."

Both my friends gasped properly.

"And that's not all," I told them bitterly. "She's got a kid, too."

"Oh, yik!" exclaimed Joann, not to be outdone.

I had to run to keep up with them because they had started to walk faster. I had it—the sympathy I needed. I could always count on these two, I thought smugly.

"It means I lose my workroom," I told them, enjoying their groans.

"How soon will this take place?" Joann asked as we entered the driveway of the Rest-Awhile at last.

"In just two weeks," I said, watching them shake their heads in deep remorse for me.

"How old's the kid?" Tina asked, shaking out her sandals. I took off my beach walkers and shook them, too. Mr. Bronstein hated sand in his motel office.

"Don't know," I said, feeling a little like a martyr. "It doesn't really matter, does it? It'll be awful. Not only will that room be taken from me, but he's bound to be a real drag! I won't be able to have any private conversations on the phone. I'll have to make sure I'm completely dressed now when I run down the hall to the bathroom. My mother and I won't even be able to fight comfortably. . . ."

We stood before the motel sign-in desk, and from behind the counter, Mr. Bronstein glared down at us. He must have been seven feet tall, and five feet wide at least.

"Sand Sweepers, you're sixteen and a half minutes late," he boomed.

They say hard work makes you forget your troubles, and for the next four hours we worked like slaves, but I never forgot for even one moment how much I disliked Cliff Morrow—and I hadn't even met him yet.

Chapter 3

Tina, Joann, and I had been sweeping sand, washing windows, wiping up floors, shining mirrors, and washing down walls for about two weeks before the day when Cliff Morrow actually stood in front of me, his pretty mother practically pushing him through the front door. And I'd never been so shocked in my life.

Cliff Morrow—in the flesh—the boy I was going to hate, stood before me, his head just clearing the door frame, his shoulders in a slump, his long, thin hands on his slender hips. His mother had to nudge him to shake hands with my mother and then with me. When it was my turn, I held out my hand, and he took it. This was no little boy—Cliff Morrow, as I was soon to learn, was seventeen years old!

As much as I hated the fact of his presence, I couldn't help but inspect Cliff the way I would any boy his age. His hair was a nice, corn-syrup blond, and his eyes were blue-gray. But his nose had a bump in it, and he had just about the most prominent Adam's apple I'd ever seen. You could actually see it ride up and down in his skinny throat when he swallowed. His ears were too big—well, maybe not too big, but they stood out a little more than they should have.

I looked pretty awful myself in my white mustard-stained shorts and an old, torn shirt, but I'd been cleaning bookcases and was not dressed to impress. Besides, I'd had no idea, since I had refused to discuss the situation with my mother, that the person coming to invade my territory would turn out to be this fairly pleasant-looking guy whom, under normal circumstances, I'd probably fall in love with. Nor had I expected him to be older—by a few months—than I was. But none of this changed the serious fact that he'd be living in my precious work space. It took all my strength—not to mention the glaring look my mother shot at me—to return the friendly smile he gave me when our hands met.

Mrs. Morrow was almost as pretty as my mother but stood only about five feet tall. How could a woman her size have a boy so tall and gangly? I wondered, as I gave her my most polite smile. She clasped my hand tightly and smiled back.

"It took only one trip with the U-Haul," she explained to my mother. "My friend Joe Angus and Cliff are helping me, so there's no problem." She glanced behind her through the front window. "I didn't know if we should pull up on this front road or go around to the dirt road, but then there would be all of that sand."

My mother raised her hand. "The front's fine," she assured Mrs. Morrow.

Without saying a word, Cliff turned and stepped out on the front steps, heading for the rented trailer parked in the driveway. I peeked out the window and saw a dark-haired man leaning against Mrs. Morrow's blue Ford, which was attached to a trailer. For a few seconds I just stood there and watched as the tall, skinny boy and the man lowered the back of the trailer.

Slowly I walked up the stairs to the second floor and then headed down the hall to the room my grandfather had added on. It would be my last few moments in there before Cliff Morrow dragged in all of his belongings. I hoped he would be careful and not paste posters on the walnut-paneled walls or pound nails in them. It had taken Grandma and me the full two weeks to clean it out, and now it looked so bare that I could have cried.

All the built-in shelves were completely empty, the dark brown carpeting had been shampooed, and new gold drapes had just been hung the night before by my mother. She had also had Russell Byron, a man she dates sometimes, hang a swinging lamp in the corner so that the desk would be properly lit.

I had spent so many happy hours in here with my grandfather that it was unreal to me that someone else would use it now. I opened the big picture window my grandfather had installed, letting in the cool ocean breezes. For just a fleeting moment I pictured my grandfather, in his chair before that window, his hands busily at work at one of his many paintings of the ocean. Why did he have to die? I thought irrationally. Just so some dumb boy could come in and take over?

I took one more long look before I heard the sound of the two male voices. They were dragging up a three-quarter-sized mattress and box spring, the older man barking directions to Cliff, who grunted in response.

I stepped back further into the hall and then disappeared into my own bedroom. What a mess! The top of my chest of drawers was jammed full of jars of creams and other cosmetic preparations. Some of the tops had not been screwed on too well, and the sides of some of them were a little smeared. My books on cosmetics and chemicals were piled between my bed and my desk, which was overflowing with more jars and more books. My stuffed-animal and doll collection fell right out on me when I opened the closet door. Mom had been after me for years to get rid of it, but there were too many good memories tied up with each animal and doll.

I'd been able to place most of my tiny saucer and cup collection on the window sill—the window that overlooks the ocean—but I knew there were still more pieces hidden away in the back of the closet in a carton that also contained my miniature prizes from bubble gum machines. My seashells were just kind of placed here and there throughout the room. From where I stood by the window, I could look back at my bed and see one sticking out from under the yellow dust ruffle.

My eyes settled on the clown picture I'd finally placed over my bed. The year my grandfather had painted it, I'd wanted to dress up like a clown for a Halloween party at school, and my mother had said that if she could find a picture to go by, it would be easier to make up my face. That's all it took for my grandfather to pick up his brush and begin to paint what would become my most prized possession. Whenever I'd look up at it, it made me feel good to realize that my grandfather was a great artist—to me anyway.

The sounds of Cliff and that other man debating over the best way to move a reclining chair into what would be Mrs. Morrow's bedroom brought me back to reality. Then I heard Mrs. Morrow and my mother in the hallway, offering their suggestions for getting the piece inside the room. Finally the deed was accomplished, and the two women went on to discuss the best place for Mrs. Morrow's chest of drawers.

I should be helping, I thought, lying crossways on my bed. But, on the other hand, if I helped I would be approving this whole intrusion. Why couldn't we have gone along just as we were? I knew the answer, of course. We needed the money.

Grandma had even volunteered to go back to work, but my mother wouldn't think of it. My grandmother had been a chemist at Cinderella Labs, makers of cosmetics. She was the one who had lured me into the study of skin care and the possible uses of natural foods for the making of cosmetics. Up until the time she retired, I hadn't been interested at all, but once she was home all of the time I saw firsthand how she was able to combine everyday ingredients into useful and effective products. But I have to admit that what really hooked me was the "secret" cream she concocted to make my freckles disappear. Later on she showed me how to make a deep-cleansing face treatment, her formula for acne, whole body treatment baths, and creams for dry skin and oily skin.

"You could have a real career," my grandmother said one day, filling me with excitement. "You'll want to bone up on your chemistry," she added, thinking, no doubt, of the C on my last report card, "even if you concentrate on working with natural foods. Our whole body is a study of chemistry."

So I bought the books my grandmother suggested, and I bought empty jars and bottles at the pharmacy downtown, and together we experimented, laughing like crazy sometimes at some of the mistakes we made. Mom laughingly referred to us as witches working up our secret brews. We always worked in the kitchen because Grandma said she didn't want to climb those "awful" stairs to go up to the room where I did a lot of experimenting on my own. Sometimes we really messed up, and we had to throw away a lot of mixtures that at first we thought might be good. But most of the time we were successful.

The only problem was that now I'd have no room for my concoctions. *He* would be living there now. For a second that image of Cliff Morrow by the front door flashed before my eyes, and I shook my head in an effort to make it disappear. If only the real Cliff Morrow could disappear as easily.

Chapter 4

I must have dozed off because the next thing I knew, my mother was knocking on my bedroom door.

"Grandma wants you to help her prepare lunch," she called to me.

I yawned and stretched like a cat and then bolted upright on my bed. The ocean was still there, out my window, the waves rolling in like clockwork, my room was still a mess, and I hadn't solved anything. Cliff Morrow was still living in my workroom.

I walked over to my dresser mirror and pulled a brush frantically through my tangled hair. The least I could do was try to look presentable, I thought. I had this crazy idea that if I looked neat and acted on my best behavior, my mother would look on me as a responsible young adult and listen to my arguments about saving my workroom. Then, seeing how she'd be ruining my future career as a cosmetics chemist, she'd have no choice but to ask the Morrows to leave. It was an act of desperation, I knew, but I had to give it a try.

Before leaving my room, dressed in my best pair of shorts and a new tank top, I spotted Cliff sitting on a mound of sand on the beach outside my window. His back was facing me, and he held a long stick with which he was drawing or writing something in the sand. He'd removed his T-shirt, and his back was so white it was obvious that he hadn't spent much time out in the sun. Once in a while he would tip his head back, his face toward the sun, as though he were trying to absorb as much as he could while it was still up there.

Diligently he worked with the stick, occasionally brushing out what was there and then beginning the process all over again. Whatever it was, he was working hard at it. Though fascinated by this sight, I couldn't help but come to the conclusion that Cliff Morrow was a strange one. The sooner he was out of the house the better.

Grandma was busy making tacos and burritos, my favorites, when I entered the kitchen. "Umm," I breathed.

"Here," my mother said, shoving a stack of plates into my hands. "Set the table for five."

Five of us, I thought. The dishes would be a project. If I couldn't get Mom to ask the Morrows to leave, maybe I could at least convince her of the wisdom of buying a dishwasher. Some good had to come out of all this.

Just then Cliff came through the back door,

walked through the kitchen, and went upstairs. A few minutes later he returned. He'd wet and combed his hair.

"Can I be of any help?" he asked my grandmother.

"No, Cliff," she told him, smiling. "But I must say it is delightful to hear a male voice in this house again."

Mrs. Morrow came into the kitchen, too. "I smell something yummy," she told my grandmother. Bending down to smell the burritos she asked, "What are they?"

My grandmother laughed. "Oh, yes, you've only been in California for what—two months? You've got some great surprises in the food line."

Mrs. Morrow followed my grandmother into the dining room, where my mother was placing a glass of water at each setting. My mother directed us to the seating positions, which, over a period of time, would become permanent.

"If we all have the same places each time, it will be easier," she said. She positioned herself closest to the kitchen door so that she could serve easily. Mrs. Morrow sat to her left, having the entire length of that side to herself. My grandmother sat at the other end of the table facing my mother, with Cliff and me on my mother's right.

Grandma picked up the huge platter of tacos and burritos and started to pass them around. She offered them to Mrs. Morrow first, who delicately removed a burrito from the platter with the server and then with the tongs picked out a taco.

"The hot sauce is over by Trish," my grandmother said, gesturing toward my mother, and Mrs. Morrow said, "Thank you."

It was like we were in a movie or up on the stage in a play with all the thank yous and excuse mes and if you pleases. I was hoping in time we could be less formal, but then maybe my mother would listen to my reasoning at last and have them leave. Or maybe Mrs. Morrow would get tired of California and move herself and her son back to Philadelphia.

The only thing I knew about Philadelphia was that its name had caused me to lose a spelling contest when I was in the sixth grade. From that day on, I hated the place. Such a long word, so terribly formal, the place could only be a haven for snobs.

The platter had worked its way around to my side of the table. I took two tacos and one burrito and then handed the platter to Cliff. Even looking straight down into my food, I could see out of the side of my eye. He slid the server under the burrito, but I guess it wasn't quite far enough because just before the whole thing slid onto his plate, one end of it collapsed. He stared down at the mess on the tablecloth as if he'd caught a dead fish. My grandmother laughed.

"A little tricky, dear," she said. I stifled a laugh. What a fumblehead! Reaching over, my grandmother helped him slide the rest of the burrito onto his plate, which was by now a mess of red sauce.

"You must have one of the tacos, too," my grandmother said. I turned and looked at Cliff's face, which was miraculously turning from bleached white to a deep red.

I looked down at my plate again, my neat plate where my tacos were sitting properly and my burrito was behaving well on the other side, before letting my eyes wander over to watch Cliff try to get the stuffed taco onto his plate.

We all held our breath while Cliff held the tongs and positioned it on the taco. So far, so good.

I thought I heard him breathe a sigh of relief when he picked it up and slowly pulled it toward his own plate. And then I watched with horror as the whole thing collapsed in midair. The cheese flew all over the tablecloth first, the skinny wedges of tomatoes and lettuce, the shower of finely chopped onions, and the crumbled ground beef.

My grandmother laughed again, and my mother gave a shaky, nervous laugh. Then Mrs. Morrow joined in. But it was strange, as soon as I started laughing, too, my mother raised her hand to silence all of us.

"Here, let me," she said, leaving her place at the table. "I'll get you a clean dish and napkin."

She helped Cliff clean up the mess, and in minutes she had returned from the kitchen with a clean plate for him. With a flick of the finger, she picked up a new taco, slid it onto his plate, slid the server under a fresh burrito, and we all started out all over again.

He was trying, I'll give him that. He poured hot sauce on the taco, then attacked it. But he clutched it so hard that the shell cracked, and more stuff fell out. It covered the burrito. But he kept eating.

Finally, he washed it all down with water. Then my mother brought out the iced tea. No sooner had she sat that down than he gulped that down, too.

"It's the hot sauce," he said in a funny, rasping voice. "I—I guess I'm not used to it."

I couldn't figure that out. I'd eaten hot sauce most of my life, and it had never bothered me.

"You don't have tacos and burritos in Philadelphia?" my mother said.

"Oh, I'm sure they do someplace," Cliff answered in that funny voice again. "But I've never eaten them."

"What he's saying," Mrs. Morrow went on, feeling sorry for her son, "is that we eat a lot of hamburgers and sometimes hot dogs. And then there's pizza. I guess tacos are more common here, Mexico being so close and all."

My mother smiled and graciously said, "I can make you a hamburger, Cliff, if you'd enjoy that more."

"No, no," Cliff answered, having found his voice again.

My grandmother reached over for the iced tea pitcher and quickly refilled his glass.

Mrs. Morrow and my mother started talking about the good weather for June, and the rest of the lunch was more or less small talk. Cliff and I said nothing, each of us casting occasional furtive glances at each other. Finally it was time to clear the table, and all of us bumped into each other trying to get through the kitchen door with the dirty plates.

"Trish, let the kids do the dishes," my grandmother suggested. "You two have a lot to do upstairs, and I'd like to lay down for my afternoon nap."

My mother and Mrs. Morrow agreed, and before I knew it, Cliff and I were in the kitchen alone, the pile of red-splattered dishes surrounding us. My grandmother had already put the tablecloth in a basin of cold water in a corner of the kitchen. It would soak overnight so that we could throw it in the machine the next morning.

I filled the dishpan with hot, soapy water and began to do the hard work, while Cliff leaned against the kitchen stool. Silently I handed him a dish towel, my eyes glued to the window, watching the sea roll in. The waves were huge today.

One by one the dishes piled up in the drainer, and Cliff proceeded to dry them and stack them on the counter because he didn't know where they went from there.

"I've got to leave soon," he said, and his voice startled me. He had been quiet for so long, but then I hadn't been exactly talkative either.

"Where?" I asked him, not particularly caring.

"Last week, after my mom told me we'd be living here, I got myself a job in Benny's Bake Shop. It's about six or seven blocks from here."

"Yes, I know where that is," I told him flatly.

"I'm going to be making donuts," he added. "Benny does all the other things."

"You know how to make donuts?" I said, amazed that a guy so clumsy when it comes to tacos could handle baking.

"You don't have to know," he stated authoritatively, having sensed the note of contempt in my voice. "He showed me. You just add liquid to the mix, put the dough in a contraption, throw the stamped-out pieces in hot grease, watch the temperature, take out the donuts when the cooker says they're ready, place them on trays, and then sprinkle them with the different premade toppings. Shouldn't be too big a deal. I bet even you could do it."

I ignored that last remark. "Good luck," I said gallantly. I hoped he liked the job so much he'd spend all his time there and I could forget he even existed—for a little while.

"Thanks. But I don't expect to be working there too long.

"Oh, no?"

"I'll be leaving soon," Cliff said, really smiling for the first time. "Anytime now my father is going to send for me, and I'll be heading back to Philly. See, I would have stayed with my father from the very beginning, but, well, he's been moving around a lot, trying to find just the right company to work for—he's into computers. So, anytime now I expect to hear from him."

A beam of hope shot through me. "You mean you won't be living here?"

"Right," he said, finishing off the last pan. "You won't have to put up with me for too long."

So he could tell I didn't appreciate his arrival. Oh, well, I thought, it didn't matter anyway.

Quickly I wiped up the counters, a new burst of energy flowing through me. I'd be getting back the little room. Mrs. Morrow would hang on, of course, but maybe, if we were lucky, she'd find a place of her own after Cliff left. And maybe by that time the Sand Sweepers would be doing well, and I would be able to contribute so much to our household that my mother would give up the idea of renting part of the place out. I wouldn't have to make my last-ditch plea to her after all.

He looked down at his watch. "I've got to go." He turned once more and looked at me with the most puzzled expression I'd ever seen on a boy. For a second I wondered if my blouse was buttoned properly, but before I could check, he was out of the kitchen and flying down the hall toward the stairs.

Slowly I wiped my hands on the same towel he had used for the dishes and then hung it on the towel rack. Opening the back door, I stepped out on the sandy wooden stairs and breathed in the wonderful ocean air, a faint, faint odor of fish drifting to my nose. I leaned on the back porch wall and closed my eyes, letting my day-dreams take over. I'd be getting my room back!

I opened my eyes just as Cliff streaked by on a red and white ten-speed, heading for the bakery. The dirt road swirled into dust behind him, and then he was out of sight.

Slowly I walked down the porch stairs, shaking the sand out of my sandals as I walked. Then I took them off and carried them with me to the sandy beach across the road. It would do me good to walk a while in the sand. The two tacos and burritos now lay heavily in my stomach.

The sun slid behind a cloud and stayed there as I bent over the spot where Cliff had been laboring with the stick. I bent down even closer and then finally fell to my knees to study it even further.

It was a face, delicately etched in the sand, protected by the wind by a bush of tumbleweed, too far up on the mound to be trampled by jogging feet and too far from the ocean's edge to be wiped out by the water. It was a girl's face. A girl with her hair tucked into a scarf. Me. I was thankful that he hadn't put in little dots for my freckles, but I was puzzled as to why he had bothered to sketch me in the first place.

I looked down the road where Cliff had peddled by in such a hurry to get to his new job. But he was nowhere in sight. Funny guy, I thought.

Chapter 5

"If I see one more horror movie, they'll have to carry me away in a basket," Joann groaned as we left the theater that night. "The only interesting thing there was Saint and Linda."

"They should go to drive-ins only," Tina added, noting how they had their heads pressed together for the entire movie.

I despise the old cliché, "I wanted to run my fingers through his hair," but that's exactly how looking at Saint during the movie made me feel. His hair looked soft, thick in just the right places, a rich black-brown, nestling around his well-sculptured ears. I'd seen those ears only from a distance, but I knew they were gorgeous.

Benjamin St. Clair, or Saint as we called him, had a rich, golden-hued tan, even in the winter. The kids who knew him said he went surfing every morning at five-thirty no matter what the weather was. He had a permanent carrier attached to his car for his board, and some of the guys at school said he was just about the best surfer around.

I often wondered why he played football. He had such a gorgeous face and body that I was sure his mother must be worried sick that he'd injure himself. But he played, and in September he'd go back and be a star quarterback while he finished his last year at Sandcastle High.

As I said, he looked great from the back, but the front of him was even better. I closed my eyes during the horror movie, not missing a thing really, and concentrated on Saint instead. There I saw his dark, dark shiny smiling eyes, his perfect nose, the unmistakable cleft in his chin, and his mouth in a smile that could knock a person flat.

"Um-m-m," I said out loud, then coughed with embarrassment midway through the movie.

"What?" Joann asked, dropping a few kernels of popcorn on the floor.

"Oh, nothing," I said, glad that she couldn't see my face in the darkened theater. "I was just thinking how great it would be to stop in Joe's for a chocolate malt."

"Do you know how many calories are in a chocolate malt?" Joann asked too loudly. Someone behind us told us to shut up.

I glanced sideways at Joann and shook my head. I mean she was a real toothpick—and worried about calories of all things! I was on the skinny side, too, but I had to really work at it. A few summers ago, I didn't know that, and I went on an eating binge, and by the time school started again, even my best friends were commenting on how I had "filled out." From that time on I felt guilty about eating, but somehow tonight I craved a chocolate malt. I guess it was my way of working out my frustration of having to watch Saint and his girl, Linda. I had a permanent crush on him—but then again what girl at Sandcastle didn't?

I sighed and went back to the movie. Huge, green, slimy grasshoppers were covering the earth, crawling slowly out of dark holes in the wheat fields. A farm girl with pretty, blond, flowing hair screamed and ran for the barn as the long-legged creatures slowly followed her. A guy who looked something like Saint dropped a match to the ground, attempting to burn the fields, but a wisp of wind came along and blew it out before he could get a fire started. The guy then ran after the girl. They were going to try to hide in the barn.

"Who cares about the grasshoppers?" Tina whispered. "I'd just like to be with that guy in the barn."

Some kids in back of us told us to be quiet again, and Tina made herself smaller in her seat. Joann only sighed.

"Rot," she said.

The whole movie was over before I knew it. At the end all the grasshoppers died—but then from the smoldering ashes out came two tiny, slimy grasshoppers. Right before our eyes we could see them slowly growing. I decided they would be having a sequel.

The lights went on, and we all started to shuffle through the popcorn and spilled Cokes on the sticky floor. My foot caught on some chewing gum, and it took me a few seconds to get out of the crummy aisle. By the time I looked up, I'd lost sight of Saint and Linda.

"Why do we spend our hard-earned money on this?" Joann said to no one in particular.

"How about that chocolate malt now?" Tina suggested.

"Okay, okay," Joann said, "but let's not fool around too long, or we'll miss the last bus."

Joe's Old-Fashioned Ice Cream Parlor was packed with the Saturday night crowd. It was the only place in our town where you got your money's worth in the way of ice cream, and even the out-of-towners knew it. Joann, Tina, and I stood in the crowded doorway for a few seconds until we saw a group of four people leave. Then we raced for the booth.

"Hi," I said to Don Pierson and his girl, Martha Brown. We exchanged greetings and waved to a few people we knew, but most of the crowd were summer people.

Tina ordered a chocolate malt, and I did the same, but Joann chose a hot fudge sundae. She would, I thought, in between wondering where Saint had gone with Linda.

"Like I said," Joann went on, "if we fool around too long, we'll miss the last bus, and then we'll have to walk."

"I love to walk," Tina said, watching Mark

Evans kiss Rita Langley's ear in the booth across from us.

"I love to walk, too," I said, "but my mom really worries when the last bus goes by the house and I'm not on it."

"I hate walking," Joann said, flipping back her blond hair. "I can't say my parents would be worried if I didn't come home at a certain time, though, especially not my mom."

Tina and I gave her our full attention.

"She wouldn't?" I said.

"No way," Joann said and smiled, making her eyes narrow slits. "She thinks that by now I should be flitting all over the place with just hundreds of boys."

"You're kidding," Tina said, making noises with her straw in her empty glass.

"In fact," Joann said, putting on fresh lipstick, "she thinks I'm out with Ken Marks right now."

"Wow," Tina said. "How did you get a date with Ken Marks?"

"I didn't get a date with him, silly," Joann said, making a face. "I just said I did, and she believed me. It kind of makes her happy."

"Won't she ask you about the date?" Tina asked, leaning on the table with both elbows.

"Sure she will, she'll even be waiting up for me," Joann said, wiping her long fingers on her napkin.

The waitress came over to ask us if we wanted something else. We all shook our heads no, and I could hardly wait until she left our booth.

"And what will you tell her?" I asked, hardly breathing.

"Lately it's whatever we've been doing together. Like if we go skating down at the Balboa Pier, that's what I tell her. Or like tonight, I'll tell her he took me to the movies."

"Doesn't she or your father ever ask to meet him?" Tina asked.

"No," Joann said. "I told them that guys don't do that anymore. I said that later on if things become serious, that's when they show up for introductions to the family."

"Oh," I said. I couldn't imagine lying to my mother about going out with someone if I wasn't.

Joann turned on me then. "Hey, how's your new tenant? The little twerp?"

"He's seventeen," I corrected her.

"You're kidding!" Joann cried, her eyes widening. "Why didn't you tell us sooner?"

"Don't get your hopes up," I said. "For one thing he's a real jerk. You should have seen how he ruined our tablecloth at lunch. Besides, he won't be staying with us too long."

"Why?" Tina asked.

"He says he's going back home—to Philadelphia or wherever his father is," I told them. "This whole arrangement is temporary. Isn't that great?"

Tina took a sip of water. "It's hard to have your parents split up," she said sadly. Tina's parents had been divorced since she was eight, and the only time she saw her father was at Christmas when she'd get on a bus and visit him in San Diego. She always came home depressed.

"But is he cute?" Joann was bent over the table, practically crawling into my empty glass.

"He's tall and skinny," I said truthfully, "and he has the biggest Adam's apple I've ever seen."

Joann sat back and sighed. "A real ugly kid," she said. "It's just as well he's leaving."

"No, no," I corrected. "He's not ugly at all. Just plain, or kind of, well, I don't know. Definitely not slick like Saint, for instance."

"Come on," Joann said then. "We've got just enough time to make that bus."

The girl at the cash register hadn't even given us our change when we saw the bus streak by.

"Well, if that isn't the pits!" Joann said.

I didn't mind. I needed the fresh air and the exercise, and I wanted some more time to talk with Joann about her phantom boyfriends. For one full block I kicked a stone along and listened to the story Joann was going to tell her mother about her "date." Then a car pulled up beside us.

"Want a lift home?" the voice called out.

My knees buckled under me. It was Saint.

Chapter 6

It was Saint all right, but it wasn't his bright red Porsche Targa he was driving. I remembered seeing this sleek white Lincoln Continental before, but always with his father at the wheel.

Saint came from the richest family in town. His grandfather owned a hosiery mill in San Bernardino, a horse ranch near Laguna Beach, a French restaurant in Beverly Hills, and a few apartment buildings in Huntington Beach and San Diego. Why his grandfather had chosen the little town of Sandcastle to live in, I'd never know. His estate sat on a hill several blocks from the ocean, but the hill was so high it towered over all those little blocks of houses, making them seem like miniature Monopoly property.

Gerald St. Clair, Saint's father, lived in a smaller, more modest home, but beautiful still. It sat further down the hill but commanded the same view of Sandcastle. I understood from my grandmother that Saint's father managed the horse ranch and was some kind of a broker. Saint was an only son of an only son, so Saint was already a rich kid.

For some reason Gerald St. Clair insisted that Saint go to public school. I'd always been happy about that decision. Saint never acted snobby, like you would think.

Take tonight, for instance. He had come upon us so suddenly, none of us could do anything but stand there at the curb with our mouths hanging open. I blinked my eyes hard and opened them again. Yes, it was Saint behind that leather-covered steering wheel. And he was alone. I wondered what had happened to Linda, but I wasn't going to ask.

"Hi," he said, his low voice curdling my insides. "Just saw the last bus go by. Can I give you girls a ride home?"

"What luck!" Joann was the first to recover. "I wasn't looking forward to that long walk!" She placed her hand on the back door on the passenger side. Saint must have touched a button inside to unlock it because before I knew it, she was climbing into the plush, deep blue velvet. A second later shy Tina followed her in.

Saint bent over the wheel and peered at me through the open passenger window. "Well?" he drawled.

I blushed and put my hand on the door handle. I could hear the click unlocking it. With shaking hands I opened the door. Somehow, my legs got tangled up, leaving me facing the wrong way. I heard Joann and Tina giggle in the back-seat, and I felt my face grow hotter, if that were possible. Then Saint reached out his arm and helped me in. I grasped it, turned myself around the right way, and sank down into the blue cloud of velvet, my breath coming hard, as if I'd been jogging ten miles.

He smashed out his cigarette in the silver ashtray on the dash.

"I've got to make a confession," he said, smiling and turning himself to face Joann and Tina. "I don't know your names, but I've seen both of you around at school. My name's Saint."

What a waste of breath and time telling us his name, I thought. Everyone knew who he was!

Joann batted her long eyelashes so hard I could swear they were making a breeze in the car. "Joann Casper," she said with a husky voice that I'd never heard before.

Saint put the tip of his fingers to his fore-head in a salute to her, and then he turned to Tina, who had sunk so far down into the velvet she looked like a small frightened kid. "Tina Morgan," she murmured so softly I could hardly hear her.

"Tina," he repeated. He gave her a salute, too, and then turned back to me. "And I believe you're Jenny Ryan, right?"

For a moment—just a split second—I couldn't remember if he was right or wrong. He knew my name! He hadn't known Joann's or Tina's, and yet he knew mine!

I could only nod my head in a yes fashion as

he started driving down the road. The music from the stereo filled the entire inside with sound. It just didn't come from up front like in my mom's car.

He touched the button on the radio. "My father's choice of music," he said, punching another button and finding a rock station. "My own car's in the shop. Dad makes me put it in once a month—when he can catch me."

"Once a month?" Tina gasped, and it sounded like it came from an eight year old. I was embarrassed for her.

"Yeah. High-performance cars need a lot of attention." He turned quickly and said, "You'd better all tell me where you live."

He talked some more about his car after we told him our addresses. I just sat there, not believing the whole thing. It seemed impossible that I was there beside Saint, riding in that beautiful Lincoln I'd seen his father in so many times.

We pulled up to the apartment building where Joann lived, and she got out. I wondered if she would tell her mother that Saint had taken her to the movies instead of Ken. "Thanks, Saint," she called loudly, sounding as if he'd dropped her off a million times.

Saint headed for Tina's. Since I lived right past Tina, I would be the last to be dropped off. The thought of being alone with him made me nervous, but I was determined not to show it.

Tina smiled and waved at us as we left her on the curb. I could swear I saw her wink at me as we drove off, and for a few seconds I felt that I had just been deserted by my friends. I had one burning question, and I had to ask it—and quickly, since my house was so close to Tina's. "How did you know my name?"

"I'll never forget it," he said, smiling as he looked straight ahead. "You had an entry in the Science Fair in eighth grade."

I nodded, remembering. I'd won fourth place that year, just missing the finals and the chance to display my project at the Los Angeles Science Fair.

"You were pushing a cream you had made from all natural foods," he went on.

"My blemish lotion," I said, smiling, remembering how successful it had been. "Yes, I remember."

"Well, it seemed ridiculous at the time." I looked over at him and *he* was blushing!

We were almost to my house. In a very low voice, he continued. "According to your display, that cream was supposed to clear pores and eliminate pimples—and I was getting some fast. Even the old family doctor couldn't control them. So I walked by your booth, I think about six times, and eventually I memorized the whole procedure. Then I hid behind the bleachers and wrote it all down in my notebook."

I looked at him in amazement.

"So I did the whole routine, with the water rinses and the steam," he went on, "and it all worked!"

He turned and smiled at me, his perfect face, perfect smile. How could a pimple even dare to think of blemishing that face!

"But, Jenny, what I've told you.... Don't ever tell anyone, okay?"

"If you had a stack of Bibles, I would swear on them," I told him. "It'll be our secret."

"I've always wanted to thank you, Jen," he said then. He reached over and touched my hands that were clutched together so they wouldn't shake.

But by that time we were home. Oh, why didn't I live further out? Why did we have to get there so fast! The white-walled tires slightly scraped the curb, and the soft murmur of the motor stopped, but he turned the key so that the music played on. The night was still, and I breathed hard, trying to remember how to exit the car gracefully.

"I've seen you around a lot," he was saying. It had to be a dream, I was convinced, and soon my mother or my grandmother would be shaking me awake, telling me I was going to be late for the Sand Sweepers.

"Jen." His voice was so deep and so terribly masculine that I could swear there was a soundtrack behind his voice. "How about checking out that new movie that's coming next week?"

Somehow I managed to find my voice. "You mean the one where the plants get so huge they destroy the gardeners one by one?"

"You got it!" Saint laughed.

I was waking slowly from my dream then. "But Linda. Linda Petrie?"

He turned to face me again, his dark eyes

44

looking into mine. Then he picked up a slim silver case that had been lying on the seat beside him. He opened it and offered me a cigarette.

"No, thanks," I said. "I don't smoke."

He shrugged, then took one out. I watched him slowly light it, inhale, and then blow the smoke in a thin swirl above his head.

"That little thing is over and done with," he said, his voice wavering just slightly. And then he turned to me again, his old smile brightening up his face.

"I'll pick you up next Saturday night at eight-thirty, okay?"

I could only breathe, "Okay."

I don't remember getting out of the car. I only knew I had to get out quickly before he looked too closely at me and realized his mistake.

"See ya." I waved to him, and he smiled his million-dollar smile again as the car pulled away from the curb. Long after he was out of sight, my shaking hand went up in the air and I whispered, "See ya," and then I lowered it and just stood on the curb in the darkness and whispered, "Yes, I'll see you again, Saint. I really, really will."

I wanted so badly to run into my mother's room and tell her the news. She'd be so happy for me, I knew. But then as I turned the key in the front door, I changed my mind. It was too good to share with anyone just yet. I wanted to float around for a day or so, keeping it all to myself. I wouldn't even tell Joann or Tina for a few days, just spring it on them Wednesday or Thursday.

A shadow moved behind me out on the walk. It was Cliff coming home from his first day of work. He must have had to work overtime, already, I thought.

"Hi," he said in a whisper. He looked tired, and the sprinkles of flour in his hair made him look prematurely gray. I laughed softly.

"What are you laughing at?" he asked almost angrily.

"Oh, just the flour in your hair," I told him and began to walk away.

"Aren't you going to ask me about my job?"

"How did you like it?" I asked politely, wanting to get to my room.

We entered the hallway together. "It was okay. But you know that Mr. Benny is not too swift on organizing things. I think he should." He looked down at me and then brushed some flour out of his hair. In his one arm he was carrying a pair of white pants and a white shirt and cap. "I've got to wear clean ones every day," he said, "and I only own one set, so until I get another, I'll have to wash these every day."

"Poor guy," I said. "Here, put them over there. I've got a wash to do in the morning."

"No, that's okay," he said. "If I don't get to it, my mom will do it." At least he didn't seem angry anymore. "Well, I guess I'll go up," he said, looking up at the stairs. "It will be funny sleeping in a new room."

"Yeah, tell me about it," I mumbled. I hoped he wouldn't wreck my grandfather's walls.

And then I thought of Saint again. Of course, Cliff didn't know Saint yet, but he would. I walked to the kitchen thinking maybe I'd have a glass of milk.

Standing alone in the dark kitchen, I couldn't help but contrast the two of them. Saint was so sure of himself, so right in every way, watching me all of those years, maybe wanting to date me, but somehow getting into a rut with Linda Petrie.

Cliff, on the other hand, was really insecure, terribly upset over his parents' breakup and not knowing where he was headed. That funny Adam's apple. So tall and thin, he was like a little boy who forgot to stop growing. There was no comparison. No comparison at all.

Chapter 7

"You have a date with who?"

We were washing down the walls in the recreation room at the Rest-Awhile when I casually mentioned Saint and my big date. Joann had responded first, nearly falling off the ladder.

Tina was a close second. "You what?" she squealed.

I repeated the words carefully now, enjoying every second of it. The words tasted as sweet as a fudge sundae. "I simply can't go to the movies with you two on Saturday night because I'm going with Saint. Benjamin St. Clair."

I continued washing the spot on the wall as if it were the most important thing in my life. Tina had been on her knees, scrubbing the baseboard. With the break of the big news, she jumped to her feet, her wet rag dangling from her fingers. "I don't believe it! I just don't believe it!" she repeated.

"But what about Linda Petrie?" Joann

asked from her position on the ladder. "He's been dating her for a couple of years."

Slowly I dipped my rag back into the smelly disinfectant and twisted the water out, all the while trying to sound like it was just everyday news. They would never know how terribly excited I was.

"That little thing is over and done with." I repeated Saint's exact words to me. "I know they seemed real friendly at the movies that night, but it was their—well, kind of like their farewell date. They both decided it had been fun but that they wanted to date other people, to expand their lives, to experience new relationships." I knew Saint hadn't said that, but if he had continued to talk of Linda to me that night, he probably would have said something like it.

"Whew!" Joann whistled, and she sat down on the top of the ladder, her wet rag forgotten beside her.

Tina threw herself down on one of the director's chairs in the corner. "Why didn't you call us? We're your best friends, Jenny!"

"Oh, it's not such a big deal," I lied, putting down my dirty rag. Actually I had enjoyed keeping the secret all of Sunday, but when Monday morning came, I just had to tell someone.

"Do you think he'll have his Porsche back from the garage?" Joann said, folding her rag into small squares, her eyes dreamy now.

"Of course he will," Tina said, crossing her legs and getting more comfortable on the director's chair.

Joann slid down the ladder to the second

step and then just sat there, her head resting back on the other steps. She sighed. "This is too much! I wouldn't even know what to wear if it was me."

"I wouldn't know how to act," Tina said, giving a big sigh.

"You don't 'act,'" I said, groaning. "You just be yourself. That's what I'm going to do, just be myself."

Tina's eyes grew larger, and she gasped, "You'll be lucky if you last through the whole movie then."

I put my hands on my hips and glared at her. "What do you mean by that?"

Tina shook her head. "Oh, Jen, don't be mad. I just meant—"

"She just meant you'd better not just sit there like a lump," Joann said from her ladder. "You'd better think ahead a little about a conversation with him so you sound interesting."

"You mean I'm not?" I was really mad now. "Boy, what friends you two are! I'll never need enemies with you two around."

Mr. Bronstein walked in just then. His face was all red, and his wheezing was terrible. "So this is what I'm paying you kids for?" he shouted. "You tell me you are going to make my walls like new pearls—and what do you do? You all relax in my air conditioning while you talk giggly girl stuff!"

As head of the Sand Sweepers, I thought I should defend us. "I'm sorry, Mr. Bronstein. It's not what you think. We were just taking a few seconds break. We'll have this done in no time, you'll see!"

Joann hurried up to the top of the ladder and began to rub the walls with her rag. Tina ran over to her abandoned bucket and resumed her position at the baseboard. It took me a few seconds to find my rag, but when I did, I turned my back to the wheezing, red-faced man and began to scrub furiously on the back wall.

I could hear him leaving through the sliding glass doors, and only when I heard the door slide firmly to the wall with a thud did I stop scrubbing.

"Wow, was he mad!" Tina said, wringing out her rag again.

"I hate this dumb job," Joann said from her perch. "Next year I want to get a part-time job in one of those classy dress shops down in Laguna Beach. Maybe one of those bikini shops."

"They won't take you unless you're eighteen or over," I said, having tried to do just that.

"That's stupid," Joann retorted. "By the time I'm eighteen, my hands will be so old-looking I won't be allowed in one of those shops."

"Wear rubber gloves like I do," Tina said.

I let them argue back and forth. I wanted to save all my thinking and strength for Saturday night because I knew they both were right, even though I hated to admit it.

I'd get my grandmother to give me another one of her kelp treatments so that my hair wouldn't be so wild. Last Saturday night Linda

51

had worn a summer dress to the movies, so I'd wear one, too. I'd just bought a white one that crossed at the top—it would make me look a little bigger there—with an elasticized waist and a slim gold belt. It would be perfect.

I'd wear my new white sandals and do my toenails a very delicate shade. But what would I do about *me?* It would take Saint only three minutes to realize I wasn't classy like Linda. I couldn't talk about sports cars, my father playing golf at the club, my trips to Europe, and my father's bank account. All I knew about were my two good friends, my mother and grandmother, and my interest in cosmetics. Maybe I could tell him about Cliff Morrow, but that would probably bore him. Maybe between now and Saturday night I could read a good book about current events—how our government was doing crazy things, how the tax situation would have to change—or maybe learn something about football.

It was strange how such a happy thought, a wonderful dream come true was turning into such a worry. Just thinking about Saturday wasn't fun anymore.

Chapter 8

On Friday morning I bumped into Cliff in the kitchen. Up until this time I'd managed to pretty much avoid him because I was always up early, dashing off to one of the motels while he always slept in so that he could work late at the bakery.

"My hours have been changed," he told me, downing a glass of milk like it was water. "Mr. Benny says he's going to hire some other kid for the donuts. He wants me to help him with the other pastries, so I'm supposed to get in there early today."

"Then he likes your work," I said, rummaging through the cupboard for the coffee. Whenever I got to the kitchen first, I made the coffee for my mother and grandmother and Mrs. Morrow. I started the coffee pot, then sat down at the table with Cliff, who by now was eating a bowl of cornflakes.

"You know, Jenny," he said, "I took the job

just for the money. But it's funny. I'm not hating it like I thought I would. In fact, I kind of like it."

"It's a good thing I don't work there." I laughed. "I'd eat everything in sight and weigh three hundred pounds by September!"

"No, you wouldn't," he said. "The first day is like that, but on the second, the smell of the stuff turns you off, and by the third day, you just don't even notice the smells. By now I can't even be tempted to taste a crumb."

Cliff helped himself to a second bowl of cereal, the coffee behind us on the counter was gurgling happily, and my own stomach had started to groan in desperation.

"Do you play backgammon?" he asked, changing the subject.

"Yes," I told him. He had hit upon one of my favorite pastimes. Last year, in fact, I'd lasted until the third day of a week-long tournament at school, when I was beat out by Mel White. All he did all afternoon was throw doubles.

"My dad and I played," Cliff said, "but that was a long time ago. Then I had this friend who I played with, but then we moved, and I haven't been able to find anyone else who's even interested."

"We'll have to play sometime," I said. Ever since I learned Cliff wouldn't be hanging around too long, my hostility toward him began to fade away. I couldn't exactly say I liked him much, but I'd found out enough to realize he wasn't a jerk or anything.

"Would you like to play tonight?" he asked.

"Can't," I quickly told him as I poured my grandmother's and mother's orange juice. "I've got to do this special thing to my hair—I mean, my grandmother has to do it."

"What special thing?" he asked. "Are you going to cut it? I think it's a nice length now."

I laughed. Most boys were so dumb about hair. "It's a special treatment," I told him. "My hair is too wavy, and the treatment helps to calm it down. We do it once in a while, especially when something very important comes up."

He finished the last bite and went over to the sink to rinse out the bowl. "Like what?" he asked.

It really wasn't any of his business, but I was so excited about my date with Saint I'd have told anyone who asked. "A date," I told him. Automatically I pulled the silverware out of the drawer and put out settings for my mother, Mrs. Morrow, and my grandmother. Maybe I'd just drink some juice and eat a donut with Joann and Tina later at our break time.

"I guess a special type of date," he said, wiping his hands on the dish towel.

"*Real* special," I said.

"Well, I guess I'd better get going," he said abruptly, looking down at the floor. "Tell my mother I couldn't wait any longer." He opened the kitchen door, and I could hear him run down the steps to the sand.

I wasn't in the kitchen alone more than a few seconds when my mother, my grandmother, and Mrs. Morrow appeared. They began to talk about a legal suit going on at my mother's office.

While Mrs. Morrow and my mother went on about the case, I turned to my grandmother and reminded her about the kelp treatment.

"I haven't forgotten," she said and smiled. "But your hair doesn't seem to be that unruly anymore." She put her hand through the back of it. "No, I think it's getting nicer all the time."

I poured coffee for everyone, and then I announced I'd have to leave. Mrs. Morrow looked so pretty in her dark brown suit, her short, straight blond hair moving gently when she tossed her head. Not many women could wear it straight like that and still look so beautiful. She was telling my grandmother how Cliff really liked the bakery, which seemed to be a big surprise to her.

"He seems to really be taking an interest in it," she said, "which is a miracle in itself. Since the divorce, he's been so low. This job is going to help him, I think."

I kissed the top of my mother's head and planted a kiss neatly on my grandmother's smooth cheek. Then I was out the door and running down the steps to the sand as quickly as Cliff had disappeared.

Right after the dinner dishes that night, my grandmother mixed up the kelp treatment and put it on my hair. At the same time she decided I was due for a facial and mixed together rice flour, rosewater, and some other stuff. It felt terrible, but she said I had to keep it on for at least twenty minutes.

After five minutes of sitting on a stool in the middle of the kitchen, I had to go to the bathroom.

"No problem," she said. "Just run in the downstairs one."

I ran to the bathroom and stopped short. "Can't," I called back to her. "Remember, Mom waxed it just before she went upstairs." I started up the stairs. "I'll be right back," I called to her.

The upper hallway was dark as I reached the top stair and went to turn in to the bathroom. After I came out, I decided to use the rest of the twenty minutes downstairs to do my nails. So I headed for my bedroom and my nail polish—and that's when Cliff came out of his bedroom.

I can't say it was a scream—not like I would scream, high pitched and shrill. It was more of a primitive wail. Cliff took one look at me and flung himself backward, hitting the wall with his head.

"Ahhh!" he cried out, and for a second I thought he'd gone crazy.

And then I remembered the stuff on my hair and my face.

"Oh, it's you!" he said. And then all of a sudden he broke into laughter, holding his sides, laughing so hard that his mother and mine ran out of Mrs. Morrow's bedroom to see what was going on.

They both shrieked with laughter, too,

when they saw me, trapped like an animal halfway between my bedroom and the bathroom. I chose the bathroom out of necessity. How dare he laugh at me! Who did he think he was?

I could hear his laughter go on and on long after Mrs. Morrow and my mother had stopped, but then finally he was going down the hall, and I could hear him laugh clear into his room and even after he closed the door.

Before I left the bathroom, I took a minute to look into the mirror over the sink. No wonder he had been in hysterics. I was a mess, a horrible, freaky mess. My hair was plastered down around my face, and my face would have scared the devil himself!

I grabbed a towel and threw it around my head because I knew I'd have to get downstairs to my grandmother, and I didn't want to be caught again by anyone.

Silently I crawled down the stairs and headed for the kitchen. My grandmother turned and looked at me, and then she began to laugh, too.

"Get this horrible stuff off me," I told her. "Come on, Grandma, it's not funny!"

And so she did, telling me how it would all be worth it, how my skin would be toned up and my hair would be soft and manageable. But I fussed and fumed while she removed the mask and then washed out my hair over the sink. Inside I couldn't help but seethe at the way Cliff had made fun of me. Why I was so concerned with his reaction I don't know, but the fact was

I was upset. Why did I care what he thought of me? He was just a nobody!

The kelp mixture was finally out of my hair, and when I ran my fingers through it, the softness took away some of my anger. My face, meanwhile, felt like a new baby's skin.

I flew up the stairs two at a time, hoping I wouldn't meet Cliff in the hallway again. And then I opened my bedroom door. I had to find my hair dryer fast. I thought it might be hiding under the dust ruffle, but in all the mess it was hard to tell. Bending down I scrounged around, and when I found the cord, I looked up and saw Cliff standing in my doorway.

He was still out in the hall but was framed in the doorway, so I couldn't really say he had actually come into my room. There was still laughter behind his eyes, and it made me madder than ever.

"I'm sorry," he ventured.

"I bet!" I threw at him.

"No, I really am," he said.

"Sure you are!" The cord was caught on something underneath the bed, so I bent over and tugged at it.

"Would you like me to help?" he offered.

"No, absolutely no!" I snapped back. I had to have that dryer, so I tugged and tugged while he just stood there watching.

"Maybe if you moved the bed a little, you could see what is holding it," he said.

"No, thank you," I said, getting madder. But the dryer wouldn't come out and if I tugged any harder, I might pull the cord right out.

I decided the thing to do was move the bed, and when he saw me tugging at the headboard, he stepped inside the room and tugged on the bottom of the bed.

Things were crashing together under there. I could hear my larger seashells snagging onto things, and I began to worry.

Finally he said, "Here, let me crawl under." He got down on his stomach and put his arms under the bed. Finally he announced, "I've got it. Here it comes."

He handed me my sewing kit—which I hadn't seen in ages. "That's not it," I said bitterly. "Oh, just go away. I'll find it. I just had it yesterday."

But he wouldn't give up. He pulled out a conch shell and then my jewelry box and then a box of jars the druggist had given me free once, and finally, at last, the hair dryer. He began to sneeze then. "It's just the dust," he said, apologizing.

I didn't need that kind of remark. "You're saying my room is dirty?" I grabbed the dryer out of his hands. "First you laugh at me, and now you accuse me of having a dirty room!"

He wasn't smiling now. "Well, yes, you've got to admit you looked like a clown with all that junk on your face and in your hair."

"It wasn't junk!" I yelled at him. "It was a hair treatment, a very good one, and the stuff on my face was a protein mask. Of course, you'd know very little about that."

"I wouldn't want to," he shouted back.

"And as far as my room is concerned," I yelled, "it was always neat and clean until you came and took my workroom. Because of you, I had to move all of my stuff in here—and now I can't find anything. And it's all your fault!"

"I didn't ask to come here," he shouted back at me.

"But you didn't have to take my workroom—and you didn't have to laugh at me!"

"You looked like a clown, exactly like a clown," he shouted, turning to go. "And do you want to know something else?"

"What, you low life? Just what else is on your mind?"

"You know something else?" he yelled as he left my room. "This place looks like a circus!"

I screamed and shoved my door shut after him, almost catching his shirt in it. I could hear my mother and Mrs. Morrow come out of Mrs. Morrow's bedroom, asking him what all the shouting was all about.

I locked the door and threw myself down on the bed, and I cried into my pillow. Cliff Morrow, go hang yourself! Thank goodness there were boys like Saint in the world.

Chapter 9

June 27. I had the day circled in red on my calendar. It had seemed that it would never arrive, yet suddenly it was there. The golden rays of light were blazing in my window, and I pushed the window open and let the ocean breeze wash my face.

I flipped on my little radio. "Good air quality," the man with the deep voice was saying. I could have told him that. The day didn't dare to be anything but perfect!

I heard a scraping noise below and leaned out the window to see Cliff riding away on his bike, his bundle of white clothes clutched under his arm. I was glad he was out of the house because I just didn't need any unpleasant encounters on *my* day.

My mother met me in the upstairs hallway. She'd just had her hair cut short again, and it made her look much younger. Her eyes looked sleepy as she walked by me toward the bathroom.

"Make sure we have all the dirty clothes together," she said, yawning. "I want to get everything done early today. Ellen and I want to do some shopping at Fashion Island, and I've got a date tonight—"

"With Russell?" I asked, yawning, too.

"Who else?" she replied, closing the bathroom door after her.

My mother had been dating Russell Byron for a long time, and once in a while they talked of marriage, but usually in a joking way. My grandmother has told me that Russell Byron was a confirmed bachelor and was afraid of the "marriage trap."

But I didn't want to waste this precious day thinking of Russell Byron and my mother or his brilliant career or anything for that matter except tonight. I wanted to concentrate on tonight.

I'd carefully gone over the newspapers that week to catch up on anything that might make good, bright conversation. By carefully studying the sports pages I knew the names of all the champion tennis players and which baseball league the Angels played in and all that kind of thing.

Joann and Tina had rehearsed a few possible conversations with me, and I had come out sounding pretty good. Unfortunately, there was no way I could get out of work because Mr. Bronstein had stressed that the Fourth of July was coming up, and he wanted his place to look "just as good as all the other places." It wasn't that he had to be afraid he would have a vacancy sign up for the holidays, but he told us that the nicer the place looked, the nicer the customers.

I was really proud of the Rest-Awhile, and Joann and Tina felt the same way. It was a lot different at the Moonglow where we spent most of Tuesdays and Thursdays. The lady manager there just didn't seem to care anymore. Her husband had died two years ago, and she'd lost interest in the place and was planning on retiring soon. I didn't expect our jobs there to last much longer.

"Mr. Bronstein, I can't work too late today," I told him soon after I arrived, giving him my best smile. "I've got a date tonight, an important date, so I'd like to leave at two if I can."

He looked at me and gave me one of his rare smiles. "I'm sure you young ladies will be done by two," he said. I wondered if he was being kind or being sarcastic.

A couple of times I caught Joann and Tina taking side glances at me, acting like I was some kind of curiosity.

"You're both making me as nervous as a cat," I told them about one-thirty. "Come on, gang, work faster. I've got to get home and wash my hair."

"But your grandmother just treated it," Tina said. She put out a free hand and touched it. "You know, Jen, it really is softer and shinier."

Joann stopped scrubbing, wiped her hands on a towel, and reached out for it, too. "Umm," she said. "It smells sweet, too, really fresh." She wasn't usually free with her compliments, so I knew that my hair, at least, was going to pass the test.

Tina dipped her squeegee down into the bucket and began to rub it vigorously over the last window. "Have you decided what you're going to wear?"

"I told you about the white dress," I said, gathering up our work things. "Linda wore a dress on their last date, and I thought—"

"You thought you might want to look like Linda?" Joann chimed in. "Weren't you the one who insisted on being yourself?"

"I really don't have time to argue," I told both of them. "Let's get this stuff back to the office. I've got to get home!"

The time was six-thirty. Two more hours to go. I sat through dinner in a dream state, wondering if I should really wear the dress or maybe something else.

Halfway through the dinner, the phone rang, and my mother answered it. She came back with a message for Cliff's mother that he would be very late.

"He sounded really excited," my mother said. "Mr. Benny is trying out a new pastry machine, and they're experimenting with it."

I sighed. How dull. Well, there has to be something for everyone, I thought.

65

Mrs. Morrow smiled. "I'm so happy Cliff found such an interesting job," she told my mother for the hundredth time.

My hair looked great. Even my mother thought it had turned out well. But that wasn't what made me smile. Over dessert my grandmother told me that, for the first time, my freckles numbered exactly six.

"It couldn't have been the protein mask," she said, frowning. "It has no bleaching properties. Maybe they're just fading with time."

"I think you scared them away," my mother said, laughing, but I ignored the remark.

"You mean someday I might not have any?" I asked.

"We make no promises," my grandmother said. It was one of her favorite expressions.

At seven o'clock I started to clean up my room. I had done everything to my body that I could do to make it look good. My nails were perfect, except for the one on my index finger on my right hand. It had broken last week, but no one could really tell because I had applied a plastic nail to it with special glue. I took one more look at it. It seemed a little longer than my real ones, but it was too beautiful to file down.

My face looked clear. I had also used my mother's eyedrops to make sure my eyes were bright. I'd done over my mascara twice on the left eye because at the last minute I'd gotten something in it, and I had had to rub it.

My hair looked better than it had ever

looked, falling gracefully over my right eyebrow. The trick was to wear it so that the hair slowly floated down toward the eye. My plan was that every once in a while, I'd push it up gently with my right hand, showing off my perfect nails.

I tried it in the full-length closet mirror, and it worked fine. I used my index finger and my middle finger, slicing into the wave, flipping it back to be placed above my eyebrow again, tossing my head back with a smile. It really looked classy.

At seven-thirty my mother met me in the upstairs hall. She was rushing around, her face flushed. "I'll never make it," she said anxiously.

"Where are you going tonight?" I asked.

"Rick Peterson is giving a big party—he's the one who owns Mayflower Toys. Russ has been trying to represent his firm for ages now, and it looks like after tonight, he may get the contract."

My mother fled into her own bedroom and took one more look at herself in her vanity table mirror. I stood in her doorway and watched her. She looked stunning in a black dress, the V-neckline accenting three gold chains, the ones she wore only on very special occasions.

Quickly she put on her black sandals and then picked up her tiny bag, which she checked for her lipstick, and compact, and small brush she always takes along whenever she goes to a party or out dancing.

"I've got everything," she announced, and then she looked up and saw me. "Jenny." She sighed heavily. "You look beautiful. I love that dress on you—it's so summery." She looked down at her own dress. "Maybe I shouldn't have chosen black."

"It looks great," I told her.

"Sit down for a second," she said, motioning to her bed. "We have another minute or so, I believe." She looked down at her watch. "Let's talk until Russ gets here."

She checked her lipstick once again in her compact mirror, snapped it closed, and then just took another look at me.

"This Saint—Benjamin St. Clair—he's something special, isn't he?"

I nodded. "It isn't that he's rich—that part scares me, Mom. It's just that he's a—well, a glowing person, a real personality. For him to even say hello to me is kind of a miracle."

My mother put her head back and laughed. "Oh, honey," she said, and she hugged me to her for a second. "Why wouldn't he want to date you? You're a special, glowing person, too!"

It was my turn to laugh. "Oh, Mom, all mothers think their kids are special. Every time Grandma's tried to give me a treatment for my hair or skin or tried to improve me in any way, you always said it was a waste of time because I was okay as I was. You just don't see me as I really am."

We could hear the doorbell ring all the way upstairs. My mother jumped up off the bed and grabbed her purse. "Jenny," she said, and she kissed me lightly on my cheek, then gently wiped any traces of her lipstick off my face. "Have a wonderful time, but remember—you are just as good as that boy."

I watched her fly out of the room and heard her greet Russell Byron as she ran down the carpeted stairs. I heard the silence when I knew they were exchanging kisses, and I wondered if Russell Byron really knew how lucky he was.

At eight o'clock I checked my hair again. The second show always started at nine, and Saint was supposed to pick me up at eight-thirty. I'd introduce him to my grandmother, and then we would have half an hour to get to the theater, buy some candy and popcorn, and find a good seat.

I would have sat outside on the back steps and watched the waves roll in while I waited, but the ocean air would have made my hair even more wavy. So I stayed inside and turned on the television in the living room.

Every once in a while I thought I saw a car pull into our driveway, but it was just a trick of the passing cars' headlights. It was starting to get dark enough for people to turn them on.

At eight-fifteen I checked my nails again. Still perfect. Quickly I ran upstairs and fumbled around in a dresser drawer until I found my breath freshener. I hadn't remembered to put it in my bag! Flipping off the lid, I squirted my tongue and then threw it into my bag. There, I had everything I would need. I went back to the TV.

* * *

At eight-thirty Grandma came in from the kitchen, where she'd been making scented soaps. "He'll be here soon, child," she said. "I never had a boy call for me early. They are always late."

"But you said you dated only Grandpa," I reminded her, my ears waiting for the ring of the front doorbell.

"That's true." She smiled and grasped my hand in hers.

At eight forty-five I decided to put all my attention on the TV show. If I didn't strain so hard to hear his car, I reasoned, he'd come more quickly. It was like the theory about watched pots and boiling water. Still, I began to worry.

At nine-fifteen, bored with the movie that came on at nine, I walked over to the window. Nothing. Then slowly I walked out to the kitchen. "I don't think he—he's coming," I told my grandmother. The words almost made me sick to my stomach.

"Oh, something just probably came up. He'll come," she said. "Don't worry, darling." But there was worry behind her eyes, too.

I sat on the high kitchen stool and watched her for a few minutes. She was preparing the lye solution.

"Your great-aunt Myra loves my soaps," she said, pouring water into a large glass jar. The lye fumes were awful. I got off of the stool and headed for the kitchen door, but then I remembered that the ocean air would ruin my hair. Quickly she flipped on the exhaust fan over the stove. "This will help," she said.

The clock over the stove ticked louder than I'd ever heard it. I knew my grandmother was talking on and on, but I couldn't seem to concentrate on anything she said.

I poured myself a glass of cold diet root beer and went back to my perch. "They were nice," I finally said. "The little soaps that looked like lemons that you made last year."

"Thank you, Jenny," she said, still stirring the lye solution. Then she went over to the kitchen table and began to measure the lard. I watched her put it in a big, enameled kettle, which she shifted over to the stove. The kitchen clock ticked loudly while I watched the fat slowly melt. Like the time that was melting away now.

At nine-thirty, while she was waiting for the lye and fat to cool down, Grandma was fussing with rose petals that she would use in her sachets. The yellow kitchen phone sat silently on its own little table in the corner. Maybe if I stared at it long enough it would ring. Saint would say, "Something came up, but I'll be right over. It's too late to catch the movie, but maybe we can grab something at Joe's and then take off our shoes and walk along the beach."

The moon was perfect for such a date. I could almost feel my stockinged toes in the sand. Maybe I shouldn't wear the stockings after all if we were going to walk in the sand. I'd manicured my toenails, my legs looked pretty good, and the sandals looked so pretty with bare feet.

"I'll be right back," I told my grandmother.

It took me only a second to take off the stockings. Now when Saint mentioned walking in the sand, I could whip off the sandals and show him that I could adjust to any situation.

My grandmother was pouring the lye into the fat and the fat was turning pink when I came into the kitchen again. Grandma began to stir again, and the fat was beginning to lighten and then become a pure white color. I wouldn't be there to see the end result, though, because I would be off with Saint.

At nine forty-five I opened the back screen door. It wasn't going to matter about my hair anymore. There were three steps down to the sand, and I sat on the lowest one with my sandals in the sand. I should remove them, I thought, but I didn't.

At ten minutes after ten the phone rang. I was up the steps in a streak, the screen door banging fiercely behind me. My hands felt clammy as I placed them on the phone and then said a feeble-sounding hello into it. My grandmother had stopped her work and was leaning against the kitchen sink.

It was Saint. "Jen," he said. His voice was soft and low, and I felt as if someone had walked up behind me and poked me in the backs of my knees.

"Yes." My voice cracked, and I swallowed hard.

"Hey, Jen," he went on, "I just got in from Catalina. Some guys and I took my boat over there this morning, and I had a devil of a time trying to get them all together to make the trip back. It was really bad, you know, the later it got the stronger those waves were and . . ."

I know the boat he was talking about—all twenty-four feet of it. I'd seen it down at the marina once.

"Rick took off for the other side of the island. He was gone so long we thought we'd have to come back without him. But then his folks would have called mine, and there would have been a big stink, and my dad would put restrictions on my taking out the boat again."

There was a long pause.

"Jen. Jen, are you still there?"

I could see my grandmother's back. She was wiping the counter, trying to look busy, wondering, I knew, what Saint's excuse would be.

"Yes," I breathed into the phone. Maybe it wouldn't be too late to take that walk with him on the beach. . . .

"Well, I'm really beat. So we're going to have to make it another time," he was saying. "It's going to be a while though, because the day after tomorrow I fly to Long Island. My mom and I are spending the rest of the summer with my family there."

"Sure," I said, finding my voice at last. "Some other time, then, Saint. . . ." My voice trailed off into nothing. There was really nothing more to say.

He said goodbye then, but I don't remember how he said it, whether it was something like "see ya" or "see you in September" or just "see you around."

The phone felt like a lead weight in my hand as I put it back on the cradle. Slowly I walked past my grandmother and opened the screen door. The air was cooler now, and the moon had slid behind a cloud.

A sudden chill shot through me as I walked down the three steps to the sand, and I hugged myself, rubbing my arms to keep warm. I should have returned to the house for a sweater, but I didn't want to go back in there and talk to my grandmother. I didn't want to talk to anyone.

Slowly I crossed the dirt road to the sandy beach, then walked with my sandals in my hand along the wet part of the sand, the cool foam darting between my toes. The cold water felt good, and I stepped closer to let the saltwater encircle my feet.

There was a pain in my chest, kind of like an aching that stayed with me all through the walk. I felt that if I relaxed my face muscles enough, tears would come, and I didn't want that. I wanted desperately to outgrow crying whenever there was a disappointment. It had never solved anything. It hadn't been Saint's fault that he was late. I'm sure he'd tried his best to get back. It was just fate. But it had been such a letdown.

I sucked in my breath and then breathed in and out hard, my feet grasping at the wet sand, my toes flexing in and out hard until they ached. I must have walked for thirty minutes before I finally started back, the moon guiding me safely back to the house.

I crossed the dirt road again and sat down on the back steps. The kitchen light was out now as Grandma had gone to bed. Upstairs the only light on was Mrs. Morrow's.

There was a towel laying on the top step. My grandmother had put it out for me to wipe my feet.

Just then I heard the scraping noise of bicycle wheels on the dirt road. Cliff Morrow. He was the last person I wanted to see now. But I had to take a second and wipe off the sand, or my mother would raise the roof in the morning. I knew my grandmother had cleaned up the mess I'd made running to the phone.

He got off his bike and approached the steps where I sat frantically wiping off the sand from my feet.

"Hi," he said too cheerfully for my mood. "Date over?"

I didn't say anything and continued to wipe my feet.

He swung around and sat down on my step. "Jenny, I've been thinking. . . . Let's make a truce, a peace treaty. I'm not saying you have to like me—I won't be around here that long—but we've both said some mean things to each other, and I figure if we both apologize at the same time we'll be even. What do you think?"

He smelled like a bakery, and I realized I was hungry because I'd just poked around at dinner.

"Want a hamburger?" I asked.

He laughed. "How did you know I was starved?"

"I know you worked some long hours today," I said. "Anyway I'm hungry, too."

He grabbed my hand. "A truce, then?"

Part of my hair was now over my right eye—in unmanageable waves instead of soft flowing ones. Casually I raised my right hand and extended my middle finger and index finger through the strands to lift it away—just as I had practiced for Saint. I might as well practice this on Cliff, I thought. Maybe by September I'd be good at it.

Cliff reached out suddenly. "You have something caught in your hair." Then his voice began to shake. "My God, Jen!"

"What?" I asked, thinking it was a horrible bug of some kind.

"My God!' he repeated, but with a terrible look on his face now. "Does it—hurt? You poor thing."

"Pull it out! What is it? Is it a spider? Cliff! What is it!" I was standing up now, and so was he.

He yanked at something and pulled it through my unruly waves. I could feel my hair catch, and it hurt.

"Your nail," he said. "Your entire nail!"

I took one look at the object he had in his hand and then down to my index finger, which was now covered only with dried glue. I lunged at him and grabbed my nail. How dare he—he should have just picked it out and said nothing!

Oh, how terribly embarrassing! I turned on my sandy feet, flung open the screen door, and bolted into the kitchen.

"Get your own hamburger," I shouted at him. "I'm not hungry anymore!" And I headed for my bedroom, my messy cluttered bedroom, where no one would be able to hear me cry.

Chapter 10

It is hard to stay mad at someone who lives in your own house. I bumped into Cliff in the upstairs hallway that next morning, as he was coming out of the bathroom and I was headed toward it. I've always been a little grumpy in the mornings, but when he greeted me with a very friendly hello, I felt like I had to mutter something.

"Hi," I said with some effort, wondering how he could smile so effortlessly at this hour. Especially when the girl looking back at him was enough to make anyone cringe—wavy, wild hair, smudged mascara halfway down both cheeks (showing exactly the route of each tear), and only nine perfect nails. What a mess! But that didn't seem to matter to Cliff, a fact that left me puzzled.

I stayed inside most of that Sunday, trying to clean up my long-neglected room. I hated to do it, but my mother had insisted I pack some of my old things and stack them in one corner of the garage. I had a terrible time choosing the things I could do without for a while.

Later in the morning Tina and Joann called, of course, dying to know how my date had turned out. I cut them both off with a brief explanation of how Saint had been delayed in Avalon, searching the whole island of Catalina for one of the guys in his group. I also mentioned that the boat had almost sunk on the way back because of the high winds and waves.

"Of course, I was sorry he couldn't make it," I told them. "But I was relieved he was all right. I think they had the Coast Guard out looking for them, too—it was quite a scare." I bit my lip on that one, but I knew Joann and Tina would enjoy the story so much more with those added embellishments.

With the calls out of the way, I finally filled two boxes and lugged the first one out into the hall to take it downstairs.

"Can I help?"

Cliff stood in his open doorway, and behind him I saw an artist's easel. My grandfather's easel!

Without answering, I stepped toward his door. "What are you doing with my grandfather's easel?" I demanded angrily. "Who gave you the right?" I knew my mother had folded up the easel and placed it far back in the walk-in closet. I couldn't believe he'd had the nerve to get it out.

"It's mine," he insisted with such force that I knew he was telling the truth. I felt deflated—

and more than a little embarrassed. It was the second time in less than twenty-four hours that I'd exploded over nothing.

"He painted in oils," I explained. "It looked just like his easel, and for a minute—"

"I would have asked for permission," Cliff said coldly, walking back to the easel as I edged further into the room to make sure it wasn't my grandfather's. "Taking other people's stuff is not my style," he said.

A large tablet of white drawing paper was clipped to the easel, and on a small metal table were hundreds of different shades of what looked like pieces of chalk. I read off shades like ultramarine blue, emerald green, leaf green—I never knew there could be so many shades of one color. Then I looked up at the white paper. He'd been sketching a face, an old man.

"I'm putting all the lines in the face now," he said flatly. He took one look at my expression and then said, "You look strange. Is it that bad?"

I could hardly find my voice. "It's just that— well, it seems so odd to have someone using this room to draw. It gives me a strange feeling in my stomach."

"I know your grandfather loved to paint," Cliff said, his anger gone. He smudged his picture, softening an eyebrow on the sketch. "Your grandmother told me. It made her feel funny, too, when she caught me sketching one afternoon."

"Except for my clown picture, he rarely ever drew faces," I told him. "Mostly landscapes. He never tired of the ocean, but he said it was a sneaky thing to get down on canvas because it was never the same. Every time he looked up it was different."

"I like faces," Cliff said. "I don't want to make a career of it or anything, but it makes me feel good. When I get upset about something, it seems to give me a little release."

"What do you want to do?" I asked, sitting down and suddenly realizing I was making myself at home, just as I had a long time ago when my grandfather had been alive.

Cliff continued to work on the face with the slim pieces of chalk. He'd draw a little, smudge it with his fingers and then a rag, and then draw again.

"That's a good question," he said. "About two years ago I would have said that I wanted to fly, and then last year I would have said something in computers—like my father's job— but my ideas keep changing."

I sat very still and watched as he put a few more lines in the old man's face. "Take the bakery. I never dreamed, never thought for one single moment, that I would do anything there except make a few dollars before returning to Philly. But Mr. Benny has really caught me up in it, really given me an interest. I think I might have found something I can really get into."

He smudged again, this time with the outside palm of his left hand. "And you, Jenny?"

I smiled. "In October you'll see what I want to be," I told him. "I believe they've already set the date for October twenty-third."

He looked puzzled, then left the easel and sat down on a black vinyl bean-bag chair. "What are you talking about?"

"About twenty years ago, a Mr. Lionel Betterton set up a special scholarship fund for Sandcastle students. The competition is always held in October—and this year I'm going to win."

"How does it work?" he asked.

I turned the chair around so that I faced Cliff directly. "Mr. Betterton always said that the most important thing in life is to have a direction and then to follow it," I began. "He believed that students who had strong ideas about what they wanted to do should try to inspire those students who are still floundering around. So he set up this whole career fair. Every year, all juniors are invited to write a few pages on why they've chosen their particular career. Then they put up booths on career day and try to sell other kids on that profession."

"Does everyone who writes a paper get a booth?"

"No," I told him. "What they do is give booths to the twenty best entries. They set them up in the gym. Like a fair. We even have entertainment and refreshments and things like that. Then the real competition begins, and the judges really get into it."

"What does the winner get?"

"That's the most wonderful part," I told him, sitting on the edge of my grandfather's chair. "The scholarship covers the entire education of that chosen career. If it's college, they'll pay for tuition, room and board, and even a little extra for expenses. If your career calls for being an apprentice of some kind, then they'll give you money to live on so you don't have to work at an outside job.

"And if the career demands that you travel—like, say you, Cliff—if you followed this baking business, wanted to study the great bakers in Europe, they'd give you the money to pay for that, too. Whatever you state in your paper, that's what the prize is."

Cliff's eyes seemed larger and brighter with my information. "It's a shame I won't be here to compete in it then," he said. "It sounds like the greatest opportunity in the world."

"I've heard of scholarships before," I told him, "But never one this great. It's one of the benefits of living in Sandcastle."

"Well," Cliff went on, "I wish I could try for it, but the way it looks now, my dad will be sending for me around the end of August. I got a letter from him on Friday. He says he is almost sure to get hooked up with this place in Trenton, New Jersey."

"That's nice," I told him. Although I was beginning to get used to the idea of having Cliff around, I still wanted this room back.

"But you still haven't told me," Cliff went on. "What do you want to do?"

"I want to do what my grandmother did. I want to create new cosmetics, using only natural ingredients. I haven't been doing much about it lately, but I've made a lot of stuff— shampoos, face creams, soaps—anything that has to do with taking care of skin or hair."

"That's terrific," Cliff said. "What kind of booth will you have?"

I always get excited talking about my future plans, so I rattled on happily. "It will have a real eye-opening banner across it. Something like 'Are you unhappy? The Ryan Ritual is your hidden key to a happier you!' And then I'll display all the cosmetics I've created out of natural foods and give demonstrations of my special facials. Tina and Joann will be my models."

"It sounds great," Cliff said, smiling. "I bet you'll even win."

"Of course I will," I told him, standing up now. I took another look at the sketch on the easel. "Why do you draw old faces? All those wrinkles?"

"I like to draw old people," he said. "Their faces are like road maps. They say where they've been, like their very own history books. It makes their character."

"People don't have to put up with lines in their faces," I said. "Someday, when we find the right formulas, people will look young for as long as they live."

"How terribly boring," Cliff said, returning to his easel.

Why did our conversations always have to end on a sour note? I wondered, getting up to leave the room. I looked around once more. In just a few months I would have the room back again, in time for my new experiments.

"Let me help you down with those boxes," Cliff said.

"No, thanks," I told him, leaving the little room. "I'll just slide them into the back of my closet. It'd be foolish to take all that stuff all the way down to the garage when I'd just have to lug it up here again after you're gone."

I turned on my heel and left him there, the chalk still in his hand, his smile fading on his lips. Maybe I shouldn't have told him about the scholarship. It might make him want to stay. And no way did I want that to happen!

Chapter 11

July was almost over when I found out the truth about Cliff's father.

It was a hot night, and even the ocean breezes drifting through the window now and then provided little relief. Tina had promised she would come over after dinner so that we could experiment with one of the facials I would use in my booth.

"What on earth are you doing?" she asked me as soon as I let her inside the back door.

"Making lipstick," I told her, returning to the kitchen counter.

"What?" Tina said, making that funny little frown with her forehead. Even with the frown, she was still pretty. If I did that, I'd win an ugly contest.

"I've been doing it for a couple of years," I said, lining up my old lipstick tubes. "You don't realize just how much lipstick you actually throw away until you go through this routine."

"I don't just throw mine away when they get too far down to use," Tina said, coming over to the counter to see what I was doing. "My mom bought me a lipstick brush, and I gouge out what I can until I just get tired of it."

"That's what most economy-minded people do," I said wisely. "But I go even further. As soon as I collect about twenty used-up tubes or ones I just get tired of, I gouge out everything in them. I mean really gouge them all out. Then I put it all into the top of a double boiler and stir it with a wooden spoon."

"It just all—melts?" Tina asked, her brown eyes growing wider.

"It has to," I told her. "Lipstick is just oil plus pigment and wax. All we're doing is melting the wax."

"Oh," Tina said, watching me stir the mixture. "But what will the color finally be? Won't it be kind of a mess?"

"Just the opposite," I told her knowingly. "Watch."

I had collected a great assortment of colors during the last year. For a while oranges had been in, then light pinks, and then a color I would say looked almost purple. The last one I'd bought had been a gold bronze. As colors melted, the almost purple one oozed into the gold bronze, and the oranges and pinks swirled together. It was kind of eerie yet fascinating, and Tina and I just stared as the wooden spoon lured them all together.

"That's absolutely beautiful!" Tina said at last. "It's a color I've never seen before."

"I call it my All Together Now lipstick," I announced proudly. "What do you think?"

"It's beautiful, but what happens now?"

"Watch." Before she'd arrived, I had washed and sterilized an old discarded jar from our medicine cabinet that I know would be able to stand the hot wax liquid. After giving the mixture one last stir, I poured the lipstick concoction slowly into the little blue glass jar.

"Now," I told her, "we'll put this jar in the fridge for a few hours. When we take it out, it will be just perfect to apply with a fingertip or lipstick brush. Now let's get on with our facial."

Tina slipped a white elastic headband over her head and adjusted it so that her hair wouldn't touch the mixture.

"I know you've said my skin is perfect," she said, "but if I don't wipe my face off with a tissue at least twice a day, it drips with oil."

"Good!" I said. "Then we're on the right track."

"How is this going to fit in with the rest of your booth?" she asked, looking somewhat worried.

"It will be great," I told her excitedly. "I'll start with you. Then when we're through, I'll do Joann. I figure with all of the other demonstrations, you'll only have to go through it twice, once at six and then again at about seven-thirty."

Tina sat down on the kitchen chair I provided for her, and I quickly wrapped a towel around her shoulders. "For you I've chosen my Paradise Yogurt Treat."

She grimaced when I applied the mixture. "How long do I have to have this glop on my face?" she asked, trying to talk through the mess.

"Keep your mouth shut. I don't want it to shift around," I told her. "Ten minutes at the most. I'll sit here and talk to you. You just nod or whatever."

She sighed and tried to relax.

"Tina," I said, "I think I'll be getting back my room soon. That's all Cliff talks about now. He says his father will be sending for him any day now. Won't that be great?"

I put up my hand then, reminding her not to respond. "Still, it's kind of funny to admit, but I think I'm going to miss him. We don't fight as much as we used to," I explained. "He's actually a pretty nice guy—I mean he works hard down at that bakery, and he keeps his room looking like one of those model homes we go through sometimes on Sundays when Mom and I have nothing else to do." Tina and Joann had met Cliff only once, and even then it had been just for a few minutes. Cliff spent hardly any time here, but when he did, he preferred to stay in his room and work on his sketches.

I looked down at my watch. "Like I said, we've been getting along better lately. We play backgammon, and we do argue sometimes doing that, but I'm getting used to him. That is, except when I want to use the bathroom, and he's in there taking an hour long shower!" Tina nodded. How could *she* know? She didn't even have a brother or sister. Except for her mother, she always had the bathroom to herself.

I went over to the refrigerator to check my jar of lipstick. Beautiful! It was getting nice and solid, and the color was unlike anything I'd ever seen in the stores. Some of the lipstick had been frosted, and it made the whole thing shimmer.

"I'll be right back," I told Tina. "I'm going to run upstairs and get my new bikini to show you, the one I bought down in Laguna last week."

She tried to smile but gave into just nodding her approval.

As I headed toward the stairs, I could hear my mother and Mrs. Morrow in the living room. They'd been watching an old Bette Davis movie, one where she has a strong southern drawl and takes away her sister's boyfriend. I'd seen it at least five times before, and so had they, but I guess they didn't mind sitting through it again. Anyway, a commercial was on, and they were talking almost in a whisper.

"I don't know how I'll tell him," I heard Mrs. Morrow say.

"Did he really leave the country?" my mother asked. That stirred my curiosity. Who were they talking about?

"Yes," Mrs. Morrow answered. I didn't want to eavesdrop, but some unknown reason kept me frozen on the stairway.

"It's so unfair," Mrs. Morrow went on. "He never wanted Cliff in the first place. He never wanted a child. He felt it was like an anchor holding him down. And me—he felt I was holding him from success, too. I gave him his freedom with the divorce. But you can't divorce a child, can you?"

"How true," my grandmother said.

"John didn't even have the nerve to tell his own son that he was leaving."

"And he expects to find freedom in Europe now?" my mother asked.

"Who knows?" Mrs. Morrow sighed. "I mean, he wasn't even going to tell *me* he was leaving. All Cliff's been talking about was his trip back to Philadelphia. I didn't want to deprive him of his father if that's what they both wanted. So I called John up to find out when he intended to send for him. But he said that Cliff must have misunderstood the letters. He didn't want Cliff with him at all. In fact, he said, he was planning on leaving in just a few days for Europe and wanted me to explain everything to Cliff."

I could feel the tears forming behind my eyes as I held onto the staircase. Cliff had been living for the day he could return to his father. What a blow that would be. I forgot for a moment that it also meant the room wouldn't be mine again. All I could think of was Cliff and how this news would shatter him.

I turned and went back to the kitchen; I'd show Tina the bikini some other time. I knew Cliff was upstairs in his room, and I didn't want to run into him now.

I went back to Tina and her facial and

hoped she wouldn't see the tears sparkling in my eyes. Turning away from her, I grabbed a yellow tissue out of the box.

"I think I'm coming down with a cold," I said.

"Summer colds are the worst," Tina said as I wiped the mess off her face.

"I know," I told Tina. Poor Cliff, I thought. I didn't want to be around when his mother broke the news to him. What would he do now?

Chapter 12

It was the hottest Sunday we had ever had in Sandcastle, the radio said that morning in early August. Tina was visiting her uncle and aunt in Sacramento, and Joann was helping her parents entertain visiting relatives, so I figured I would just poke around and maybe even work on my paper for the scholarship competition.

I could hear Cliff moving around in his room, making his bed, dragging out his easel. I wondered if he was working on his sketch of my grandmother. She'd sat for it three evenings in a row that week, until he was sure of the "flow" of it. I had to admit that so far he was doing great.

I told myself I'd check in on him later, after I tackled that scholarship essay. The rules for the essay were pinned to my bulletin board. They'd been there since last year, and I knew them by heart: no more than one thousand words, approximately two-hundred fifty on each typewritten, double-spaced sheet.

I looked at the blank pages in front of me on my desk. I had to make it perfect. It would be awful to fail the first part of the competition. Then it would all be over. Finished.

I'd have to really think, be really careful what I put down on those four pages. I figured my grandmother's influence alone would take up one whole sheet.

I sat down and thought, but the words wouldn't come. A half hour later I concluded it was too hot to write, so I decided to run down to the kitchen and do my laundry. So many things had piled up over the last few days.

Cliff came into the kitchen just after I did. "I never knew it got so hot here," he said, and he, too, was lugging clothes toward the washer. He bent down and wiped off his forehead with the edge of one of his shirts.

"I'll do them later, Cliff," his mother told him. "Right now Mrs. Ryan and I are headed for the beach. It's too hot to do anything."

"That's okay," Cliff said. "I know how to work that thing. I'll get in line here behind Jenny and do them when she's finished."

Our place was beginning to look like a public laundromat, I thought, reaching for the detergent. My washer load started to hum and churn, and I reached up into the cupboard for a glass. I needed some cold orange juice.

Cliff sat down at the kitchen table and spread the Sunday papers out in front of him. I wondered how Mrs. Morrow had explained about his father not wanting him. I had watched him closely for any change in his face or his talk. But nothing had changed. He asked his mother every day if there was any mail for him, and every day I'd watch her shake her head no. He must feel awful, I thought. I sat down at the other end of the kitchen table, sipping my cold juice, picking up a section of the paper and pretending to read it, watching him over the edge of the paper and trying to read his mind.

Cliff didn't deserve to be treated so shabbily by his father. He really had grown on me these past few weeks, something that I would have thought impossible way back in June. I'd even grown to like his nose. It really was a very acceptable one, even with that small bump in it.

Even his Adam's apple had character. My eyes centered on the top of his head as he lowered it to read the paper, the corn-syrup blond hair, just slightly wavy, falling over his forehead now. When he reached up and pushed it aside, I could see his right eyebrow. That, too, was nice and not too bushy. For some reason, though, it made me think of Saint. Of course I thought of Saint every day, every night, but it was funny that Cliff's eyebrow would make me think of him at that very moment. I knew I was comparing them, but unlike that time when Saint had won hands down, there was more about Cliff to like now. Sometimes I even wondered what a date with Cliff would be like, but every time the notion came into my head I would quickly get rid of it. It was so unfaithful to Saint to think like that.

Nevertheless, Cliff's long fingers held the pages of the paper with a strength and grace I admired. It was funny that with hands like his he liked baking. But then I guess the way a person is built doesn't have to have anything to do with the things he wants to do for himself.

"I have a great idea," my grandmother said, coming into the kitchen. "Since you and Cliff will be the only ones around for dinner tonight, why don't you get out of this hothouse and cook out on the beach? We've got hot dogs and rolls—and marshmallows, too. We have a bag of them left from Fourth of July."

Cliff looked up from his paper. "Do you want to, Jenny? I've never cooked on the beach."

"Oh, I don't think so," I said, turning the pages of the paper. "So much easier to do them on the stove."

"But not as much fun," my grandmother said.

"But the wind blows, and the hot dogs get sand in them," I protested.

"I've never had hot dogs with sand in them," Cliff said.

"So it's settled," my grandmother went on boldly, ignoring my protests for some reason. "You don't even have to go out to the store. Everything's here, even the cans of root beer."

I let my shoulders slump. My grandmother always tried to make things fun. But it was too hot to have fun today. I said as much to her, but that didn't stop her.

"It will be cooler tonight. Wait until the night breezes start. Then go down and build a fire in one of those fire rings along the sand."

"Okay, Grandma." I reached out and patted her hand. "If it will make you happy."

Grandma smiled smugly. She knew she would win in the end.

It was seven-thirty before the breezes finally stirred, making the beach bearable. Cliff stood beside me as I packed our small ice chest. Hot dogs, rolls, mustard, relish—should I take the chopped onions? If it had just been my mother and grandmother or even Joann or Tina, I would have packed them without a thought, but something strange was happening here. What if I took them and ate them and he didn't? I could see him backing away from me, my breath reeking of onions! He'd never want to talk to me again after that.

I couldn't make up my mind, though, so I threw them in with the rest of the food. I packed four cans of root beer, a bag of marshmallows, paper plates, a handful of napkins, and plastic knives, forks, and spoons. Cliff grabbed a small bundle of wood from the pile we always kept on the back porch.

We wore our swimsuits because night swimming this hot night would be perfect. I had on my blue flowered bikini, and Cliff wore a dark brown suit. We both carried sweatshirts because we knew it would eventually get chilly. I carried the picnic things, blanket, and towels, and Cliff carried the ice chest and the wood.

"Let's grab the closest unoccupied fire ring we can find," I said, struggling with my load.

"It's okay by me," he said, breathing hard, dragging the bundle of wood behind him.

We had to pass three of them before we found an open one, and gratefully we dumped our burdens. Cliff got into the business of starting a fire right away while I brought out the hot dogs and the coat hanger sticks my family had made a long time ago.

It took only a few minutes for Cliff to get the fire roaring. He started with a few pieces of paper he'd found on the beach, then splinters of the wood, and then the bigger pieces, fanning them patiently as the fire grew and grew. Then we slid the hot dogs on the wire sticks and held them over the crackling fire. Once or twice the sticks tangled with each other, and we laughed when we tried to pull them apart.

"They even tangle with each other when they're out of the closet." Cliff laughed.

It was beginning to get cool, so I slipped on my sweatshirt. Cliff grabbed for his, too, and we sat closer together on the blanket, watching our hot dogs bounce gently over the orange-red flames. I felt remarkably comfortable with him.

"Are you getting used to California?" I asked him at one point.

For a minute he didn't answer me. I busied myself getting the rolls out of the package and lining up the mustard, relish, and the onions. Then I opened two cans of root beer and handed him one.

"It's okay, I guess," he said at last. "Maybe next time I come here I can stay longer. I figure

I'll be leaving sometime before school starts. I've got to get enrolled somewhere, and I hope my dad realizes that. Of course, I could get away with not enrolling until the end of September."

"I think you'll like Sandcastle High," I said, removing the mustard lid. "We have good teachers and loads of activities—something for everybody."

I handed him his roll after I spread it with the mustard. He reached for mine, too, and quickly slid the rolls under each hot dog.

His angered expression surprised me. "Why do you push it, Jenny?" he asked, watching me spread some relish on my roll. "You know I'm leaving soon. I won't be going to your school at all. You know all of this, and yet you come right back to the same subject every time, telling me about your school, the career competition, how much I'm going to like it!"

She hadn't told him yet! It was unfair of his mother to keep the truth from him, but then maybe if I had been in her position, I would have waited for the right time to tell me, too.

"Here." I shoved the plastic container of relish under his nose. I was being abrupt, I knew, but my impulse was to tell him the truth, and I knew that was the worst thing I could do.

"Don't you have onions?" he asked, not smiling.

"I have loads of them!" I said, grabbing for the plastic container. I was glad I had packed them now. I grabbed some for myself first before I passed them on to him. There wasn't much more room in my hot dog roll, but I jammed in as much as I could. It wouldn't matter how badly my breath smelled now.

There was complete silence as we finished six hot dogs—I ate two, and he ate four. I wanted to ask him what he was thinking about, but I didn't dare open my mouth now.

Finally he slipped a marshmallow on each stick. They looked like tiny white pillows melting over the leaping flames as they turned gold and then toasty brown.

Afterward, we cleaned up the mess, folded up the blanket, and were about to throw sand on the fire when another couple came along and asked if they could use our fire. I wanted to linger just a little longer, but Cliff seemed anxious to go, and so we surrendered our fire ring and started walking down the beach, the cold water lapping at our toes.

"Let's sit down over there," he said suddenly. We threw ourselves down on a little bluff overlooking the inky-looking ocean. For a few minutes we sat there; I stared out at the neverending ripples, and Cliff doodled aimlessly in the sand.

"The wind is really coming up strong now," he said, wiping the sand from his eyes. "Look, I didn't mean to be so abrupt back there, but you just go right on mentioning school and—"

"Drop it," I said, putting up my hand to stop him. "I swear I won't mention it again. We'll just talk about something else. Or would you like to go back to the house? There's a good movie on TV tonight," I added.

"No," he said, and from the sound of his voice, I could tell there was something important he wanted to say. "This guy you're going with. I've heard some talk about him down at the bakery from Phil Banks."

"Oh, I know Phil," I said, digging my toes into the sand. "What about him?"

"I don't know what's going on, but one day Phil came in early, and we got to talking about the people around here. He said Saint comes from the richest family around here."

"That's right," I said, smiling. Even though I was with Cliff, the mere mention of his name made me wonder what Saint was doing now.

"What else did Phil tell you?" I asked, remembering what Saint looked like and wondering just when he'd call me for our date.

"I told him that you were going with him, and he laughed and said you couldn't be because Saint was heavily dating Linda Petrie."

"Was is the correct word," I said. I turned to face Cliff then, and I knew hot anger flashed in my eyes. "Just because a guy dates a girl for a while, that doesn't make them married, does it? It just so happens Saint broke up with Linda. He told me so himself." I started laughing so hard I couldn't stop. "I didn't know males gossiped!" Standing up I ripped off my sweatshirt and dashed toward the water, leaving Cliff sitting there on the blanket.

The cold water hit me like an electric shock as I ran under the waves. In seconds he yanked off his sweatshirt, too, and I could hear him right behind me, yelling and squealing that the water was freezing.

By that time my body had grown used to the sharp cold, and it felt warmer. Diving wildly into one wave and out the other and then letting the thrust of the incoming waves pull me back to the beach again, I thought of Saint.

I would have to get used to the talking, the never-ending gossip. I knew I'd better be ready for it. When two people date for so long, they almost seem to line up a group who expect them to go right on dating. People are strange, I thought, diving again into another wave. And then suddenly Cliff was right beside me.

"Careful," he said. "There's a strong undertow. Feel it?"

I had felt it, of course, but I'd been thinking of Saint, too.

"I can handle it," I yelled to him over the break of another wave.

Suddenly, like a building falling on me, a huge, monstrous wave knocked me down to the depths of blackness, and I struggled to overcome it. Flailing my arms, I tried to come up for a breath of air, but each time another and then still another wave hit me smack in my stomach. I knew I was swallowing too much saltwater.

I raised one arm straight up, and my scream came out like a gurgle. I couldn't even see Cliff in the waves that seemed to be mountains of water now. My body was being pulled out instead of back to shore. I screamed again, and then suddenly I felt strong arms grabbing me around my middle. They were lifting me up higher than the next wave, saving me from swallowing the saltwater again.

At last the strong arms pulled me through the terrible undertow that was trying to drag me the other way. I gasped Cliff's name as he tugged me along after him. I could feel his legs struggling through the water's hateful pull. And then we were up on the sand, our bodies heaving and gasping for breath. Finally I was able to stop the spasms that shook my whole body, and I sank on my stomach into the sand, the water pouring out of my mouth like a spigot turned all the way on.

I felt Cliff's strong arms on my back, pushing the water out of me. A chill hit me then, and I began to tremble and shake violently. Quickly he picked me up and carried me back to where we had left our things, and he wrapped me in the blanket.

"We'd better get you back home where you can take a hot bath and get to bed," he said, a concerned look in his eyes.

"That never happened to me before," I told him, my teeth still chattering. "I mean—I mean I could always—I was always in con-control. All these years I've been swimming in that darn ocean. . . ."

"That's a real problem," Cliff said. "Even expert swimmers have drowned that way."

As soon as I felt stronger, we picked up our things and headed for home, the lights of my house greeting us as we crossed the dirt road. For a few seconds back there, I'd thought I'd never see them again.

We dragged the ice chest and leftovers into the kitchen. I felt terrible. My hair was a tangled mess, and Cliff laughed when he pulled a piece of seaweed out of it. Quickly I wrapped a clean towel around my head.

"I want the shower first," I told him, running past him. We were in the downstairs hallway when he suddenly reached out and stopped me.

"Jenny," he said, "it was a real scare for me."

"For me, too," I said, not pulling away.

"Jenny, please be more careful. I mean you might have been alone out there."

"I will. Don't worry," I said.

His face was close to mine now, the worry showing clearly in his blue eyes. Suddenly I realized he was going to kiss me! I could feel his breath on my face.

And then he ruined it!

"Do you—would you mind if I kissed you, Jenny?"

What was I supposed to say? "Go ahead," came out of me before I could think.

"You probably have been kissed hundreds of times before," he said, smiling weakly.

"Thousands," I told him, wondering what kind of a freak I looked like, my head wrapped in that towel, my sweatshirt full of sand and saltwater. We must have been dripping on the hallway carpet, too; my mother would kill me.

"Me, too," he said.

"Me, too, what?" I asked, puzzled, not being

able to follow this crazy conversation. I started to tremble again. Maybe I'd get a cold now from being exposed to the cold water and night air.

"Me, too," he said again. "I've kissed thousands of girls in my time."

"So we should be pros at it," I told him sarcastically. I started to leave again, but he pulled me back.

He bent to kiss me, and I felt the warm brush of his lips. Not in one thousand years would I ever, ever let him know that it was my first time! It was absolutely amazing how his lips felt on mine. It would take a real poet to describe it.

My eyes were still closed when he said it. The moment had been so beautiful, but like the real klutz that he was, he ruined it.

"You ate the onions," he said, his mouth still close to mine.

"But you did, too." I couldn't believe he was saying that!

"No," he said. "I changed my mind."

I threw my head back in fury and sucked in my breath. "Cliff Morrow, I hate you!" And with that, I was up the stairs, heading for the shower.

Chapter 13

I didn't mean to let my anger go as far as it did.

Maybe I had swallowed too much saltwater. Maybe I was a little crazy. Whenever I do something really stupid, I try to think up all kinds of excuses for myself, but this time there was no excuse that I could find to justify the awful thing I did.

It happened quickly. I'd taken a long, hot shower and then crawled into bed. I could hear Cliff coughing in his bedroom for a long time before I heard my mother, Mrs. Morrow, and my grandmother talking in the hallway.

Mrs. Morrow knocked on Cliff's bedroom door and asked him if he was okay. He called back that he was fine, that it was just a little cough and nothing to worry about.

For a while his mother stayed in her room, but then she came out and asked him again if she could get him anything for that cough. He answered that he would be okay. Mrs. Morrow must have gone back into her room then, but I didn't hear her door close.

I did hear my grandmother climb the stairs and talk to Mrs. Morrow, however, and in my half-asleep, half-awake state I heard her tell Mrs. Morrow that there was some cough medicine and Vicks rub in the bathroom medicine cabinet.

I drifted in and out of sleep again. The next thing I heard was Mrs. Morrow talking to Cliff.

"Come on, Cliff, don't be a child. It's only a tablespoon, and it tastes like cherry." It sounded like something my mother had said to me a long time ago when I had had a horrible cold.

"I don't need it," Cliff said between rasping coughs. I sat up in bed. A person couldn't sleep around here anymore.

"That's fine," I heard Mrs. Morrow say. Cliff had obviously given in to her.

"Now take this," she continued. "This Vicks rub will really help you—do you want to lose work at the bakery? Do you want Mr. Benny to have to hire someone in your place?"

"Okay, okay," I heard Cliff say dejectedly.

"Here, rub it all over your chest and neck. Tonight you'll have to wear your pajama tops. Let me see, where are they?" The sound of her rummaging through his dresser drawers followed.

I heard Cliff grumble, then there was silence. I don't know how much time actually passed before the awful thing happened.

Mrs. Morrow's bloodcurdling screams pierced the entire house, waking up all of us. I shot out of bed, my legs crumbling under me because I'd stood up so suddenly. Also because I was frightened. The screams were coming from Cliff's bedroom!

I grabbed my robe and threw it around me. By this time I heard my mother open her door and run down the hallway toward Cliff's room. My grandmother, on the bottom stair, was just starting up.

I entered Cliff's bedroom first because my room is right next door, but my mother pushed me aside as she flew into the room. Taking one look at Cliff, she put her hand to her mouth and gasped.

It was my turn to look. Cliff was sitting up in bed, his eyes wide with shock. His chest was covered with blood! I turned away. Oh, my God, I thought. Something is wrong with Cliff!

Slowly I turned to look again. He cried out. "Why are all of you looking like that? What's wrong with me?" Then he looked down at his chest and let out a terrible whelp like a struck puppy.

My hands flew to my eyes. It was too much for me. But like I do in scary movies, I spread my fingers open just slightly to take another look. It looked like blood all right, but then I spread my fingers apart even further and saw a red-orange color, a little pink, and a streak that had a little hint of purple.

I took my hands clear away from my eyes when I saw the little glass jar on the bedside table by the lamp. The jar of Vicks. Somehow my jar of All Together Now lipstick had found its way into the medicine cabinet!

I can't tell you the uproar it caused. There I was trying to explain, pointing to the jar, Mrs. Morrow looking at me like I was crazy, my grandmother moaning and then breaking into laughter, my mother putting her hands on my shoulders and shaking me.

"Your lipstick? In a jar? But that was Vicks!"

I was laughing now. I really couldn't help it. Cliff was furiously trying to wipe off his red, orange, bronze, pink, slightly purple chest, and I was laughing.

Unfortunately Mrs. Morrow was not. She turned and glared at me. "What a terrible trick!"

"I didn't mean it," I said. "I don't know how that jar got in the medicine cabinet. I didn't do it on purpose!"

My mother raced to my defense. "Jenny would never do a thing like that. Besides, how would she know that Cliff would ever need it? The Vicks rub, I mean?"

Mrs. Morrow mumbled that she was sorry she had screamed at me, and then she turned to her son, who was still sitting up in bed trying to rub off the lipstick. "I'll get some face cream out of my room. It takes off makeup." She disappeared down the hall while I headed for my room.

A few minutes later I heard the two of them talking, and I crawled back into bed. But then I decided to take one more trip to the bathroom before he took it over for his shower. That's when, unfortunately, I bumped into him in the hallway.

He glared at me. I'd never seen anyone so mad before. "Boy, clown, you really scared my mother. I won't stand still for that kind of thing!"

My mother came out of her bedroom. "For heaven's sake," she said, "It's the middle of the night. You children will have to stop fighting." Her hair was tousled, and her eyes looked tired. "Look, you two will have to learn how to get along with each other if we're all going to live together in this house."

Cliff turned on his heel and faced my mother. Mrs. Morrow was right behind him. "Don't do me any favors, Mrs. Ryan. I won't be here that long. Don't even try to get Jenny to treat me like another human being!"

I glared right back at him. "It wasn't my fault, I told you. It wasn't my fault!"

"And this is the thanks I get for saving your life. Without me, you might have drowned."

My mother's head shot up. "Drown?" she said, looking confused.

"I would have saved myself!" I threw at him. "I was just making believe I was in trouble—testing you—to see if you were a good swimmer."

"You're a liar!" His Adam's apple was really racing up and down now. "I can't wait until I get out of this house now!"

"You're a fool!" I yelled. The next words were scarcely out of my mouth when I regretted them. "You go around telling everyone that you'll be leaving soon. Well, we all know your father doesn't want you—he's not even in this country anymore! You're stuck here Cliff Morrow, and you might as well get used to it!"

My hands flew over my mouth to stop the terrible torrent of words I was hurling at him. He just stood there, shock in his eyes, his chest still covered with some of the lipstick and cold cream. His shoulders slumped, and his eyes flashed over to his mother and held her gaze for a long, deadly moment.

She was the first one to speak. "I'm sorry, Cliff," she said sadly. I wished at that moment that I *had* drowned.

"He left the country?" Cliff said, disbelieving.

"We'll talk after your shower," Mrs. Morrow said, putting her arm around him. She was so tiny, she had to look up at him, and I saw the pain and love in her eyes.

Quickly I brushed past them and made my way back to my bedroom, where I threw myself down on the bed, the tears gushing out from me like waves barreling in from the ocean. They even tasted like saltwater as they ran down my face and into my mouth.

"I'm sorry," I whispered into my pillow. Cliff would be finished with his shower soon, and then he and his mother probably would talk together most of the night. She would try to give him enough love for a mother and a father. She would try to find the words to make the hurt more bearable for him.

Chapter 14

The large Sandcastle High gym overflowed with students on registration day. Tiny folding tables were set up in strategic places around the floor, the tops of them covered with tons of papers, pamphlets, and sign-up sheets. Most of them were manned by teachers and counselors, but some of the extracurricular activities were held down by seniors and local college instructors who would be lecturing at our school.

It was a mass of confusion when Joann and Tina and I entered the noisy, crowded place. All three of us had been able to complete our required rosters back in May, but if we wanted to take any of the extracurricular classes, we had to sign up today.

As soon as we entered the gym, we split up. I headed for the "New You" table with about twenty other girls. I grabbed a pamphlet that explained all about this personal appearance course I wanted to take, and then I stood at the end of the line, hoping by the time I got up to the lady who was running the whole thing, the class wouldn't be closed.

The line moved slowly, and as I waited, I looked up at some of the other lines. It figured that Cliff was the first familiar person I spotted. He was talking to Mr. Peters, one of our shop teachers. I watched Cliff gesture with his hands during the conversation, and I was amazed at how both were laughing and talking so easily together. Mr. Peters stuck out his hand to Cliff, who grasped it before heading for the new-student registration line. My heart went out to him. He was doing the one thing he always said he wouldn't have to do. It must be painful for him, I thought sadly.

After that dreadful night I told him about his father, he had just gone on as before, working long hours at the bakery, running on the beach until he came home exhausted, and bringing home flowers from the market for his mother.

Never once did he refer to that night again, and to keep the peace neither had I. We even went back to playing backgammon out on the back porch steps. There were so many times when I wanted to reach over the board and take his hand and tell him how much I hurt for him. But I never found the words. Away from our games we remained in our separate worlds, never coming close to recapturing that special moment we had shared after he had rescued me from the water. I knew now that I liked Cliff a lot, but those terrible words I'd hurled at him that night created a vast gulf between us.

His interest in the bakery was intense now—he talked of nothing else at the breakfast table. He was also spending more time with his mother. I watched them a lot lately, running together on the beach, her tiny form trying so hard to keep up with his long legs. Often he'd hold back, trying to let her catch up.

One thing I'd learned about Cliff—he didn't burden anyone else around him with his disappointments. He just carried them inside him and never let on to anyone of us. I admired that.

Joann ran toward me, waving a pamphlet. "I've got it! I've got it!"

"The dancercise class?" I asked.

"Right!" Joann said, her long hair flying in all directions. "Another five minutes or so and the class would have been closed."

"Lucky," I said, trying to see how many people were still in front of me. "Cross your fingers for me," I told her. "I've just *got* to get into this thing."

Finally I reached the front. "Hello, Jenny," Miss Lawrence said. "You just made it."

"Thanks," I told her, my face almost breaking from smiling as I signed my name to the long sheet. I took the literature she handed me and told her I'd see her in a few days.

Joann spotted an old friend she hadn't seen all summer and walked over there to greet her. I was turning away from the line, looking up from the papers in my hand when I saw him.

Saint. He was standing near one of the doors, talking to two girls I'd never seen before and showing them a picture in his wallet. It was probably a picture of his father's boat, and their attentiveness made me twinge with envy.

Then he looked up and saw me, and his face broke into smiles.

"Hey, Jen," he called. His voice sent a shiver through me.

I stood in place as if I had been frozen there. Should I walk over? Should I make him walk over to me? But then what if he didn't? It appeared he wasn't moving, just waving. I swallowed my pride or whatever it was, and I moved over toward him, but slowly so that I wouldn't seem overanxious.

The two girls left his side and went on to other things, probably wondering what glorious thing I had that they didn't.

He squeezed my hand, and I thought I would die where I stood. His hand was hot on mine, and for a second I thought my hand would melt like a piece of chocolate.

At last he let go, and I breathed again. He went on in that deep voice of his. "Hey, kid, what have you been up to all summer? Man, I'm glad I'm back! The East Coast is bor-ing."

I threw my head back in my practiced gesture and smiled at him, flipping a few strands of hair back over my right eyebrow. By this time I was perfect at it. "Just having a great, super time!" I said in a lilting voice. (I'd practiced that, too.)

"Well, now listen," he said, bending his

head to meet mine. He was just inches away from my face; another inch or two and our mouths would have touched. I could feel the warmth of his breath, smell the delightful peppermint gum he was chewing with his gorgeous teeth.

"I'm going to be a little busy—football practice and everything—and you know what the senior schedule is like. I just wanted to let you know I didn't forget our overdue date."

"No problem," I told him. "I'm really going to be super-busy, too—the career competition and all."

"You're going to enter?" He seemed surprised.

"For sure!" I said, smiling my sweetest smile. I flipped my hair back again. "Just whenever you do get time, Saint, give me a call, and we'll see what we can set up."

I left him standing there. I knew he would call me now because I hadn't fallen all over him. I'd read in one of those *Cosmopolitan* magazine articles, "Walk away first, don't ever let him walk away from you." It was information on how to conduct yourself at a cocktail party, but I knew it would work well in any crowded situation.

Trembling almost uncontrollably, I searched for Tina, finally finding her in the home decorating line. What on earth was she doing there?

Quickly I walked up beside her. The kids behind her glared at me as if I were trying to cut in.

"Aren't you in the wrong place?" I asked her, my knees still knocking.

"No." She smiled. With her hair tied back with a blue ribbon, I swear she could have passed for a freshman.

"When did you get interested in this?" I asked her.

"Oh, I've always been," she said, inching up with the line. "It started seriously this summer," she went on. "Remember the Victorian dollhouse my uncle made for me, the one I brought back from Sacramento last month? I'm going to wallpaper the whole inside and fix up each little room, and I figured this would be just the class for me. Maybe I'll learn something."

I remembered the day Tina had shown me the dollhouse, a really huge house designed for a dollhouse collector. It had been a serious project of her uncle's, and I had been overwhelmed with its beauty.

By the time Tina was finished, Joann had caught up with us again.

We left the gym behind us, our pamphlets and all our pieces of literature tucked under our arms. We headed out to catch a bite to eat before going to work. It was to be our last day at the Rest-Awhile.

"I saw you talking to Saint," Joann said, taking huge strides with her long legs. I was having a hard time keeping up with her, and Tina was practically running.

"Yes," I told her. "We're, well, we're trying to get together, but we're both so busy—"

Joann turned to face me. "Hah!" she said and threw her head back in a laugh. "Come on, Jen, what did he actually say to you?"

"You know perfectly well how busy I'm going to be," I said, quite clearly. "The career day is next month—exactly forty-four days from now. My paper has to be in on October fourth. That's exactly twenty-five days from now."

"Oh, Jen, that reminds me," Tina said, finally catching up to me. "I can't be in your demonstration."

"What?" I said, coming to a screeching halt. "Why not?"

"Because I'm going to enter the competition, too," Tina said, smiling weakly at the two of us.

One of my best friends competing against me! I gasped, and then I laughed at myself. I should be proud that she had found a true direction and wanted to interest others in it.

"What will it be about?" I said, walking toward the good smells of Taylor's hamburger stand.

"Interior decorating," she said simply.

I wanted to say, "But what do you know about interior decorating?" But that would have been cruel. "Great," I said instead. "Hey look, Tina," I added, "if you want some help, I know my mother has some books on it. She was interested in it, too, at one time."

Tina smiled as she dug down in her jeans for her money. "Thanks, Jen, but I'm pretty well set. I appreciate it, though."

Joann and I looked at each other over her head. I'd never suspected that little Tina would enter anything.

Chapter 15

I finished my career paper on Thursday, October 1. It wasn't due until the following Monday, but I was relieved to be done with it. Now I could go on and actually plan my booth because, of course, I would be one of the twenty chosen for the displays. I'd read that if you actually see yourself winning, you stand a better chance of having it come out that way.

Friday was a free day for the students at Sandcastle High. Every year in early October, the teachers hold a full day of meetings, trying to iron out problems, so we got the day off. Having been kept prisoners in school since the second week of September, we all felt we were long overdue.

Sitting next to Cliff at breakfast, I found myself feeling sorry for him. He was working evenings in the bakery now so that it wouldn't interfere with school hours. He would only have a free day until five o'clock.

I was just starting to make my bed when the phone rang. My grandmother answered it and called up the stairs that it was for me. It was probably Joann or Tina, I thought, as I walked into my mother's bedroom and picked up the extension. We had left our plans up in the air because Joann couldn't seem to make up her mind if she wanted to go swimming or shopping down in Laguna, and Tina couldn't decide if today was the day she'd stay home and do her career paper. She hadn't even started yet!

My one hand that was resting back on my mother's bed suddenly clenched into a ball when I heard his voice. Without realizing it, my nails dug hard into the palm. His voice was clear and deep, bringing back memories of his heavenly face.

I had hardly seen him since that day in the gym, except in the hallways at school and, of course, out on the football field. He'd always been surrounded by girls or football players. There had been no space for me, and I was beginning to think that everything he'd said to me had been part of a cruel hoax.

"Jen, I've got a terrific idea," he began. "My folks have this cabin up at Big Bear. They're fixing up the place for a grand reunion on Thanksgiving, and someone has to be there so the gas man can come in today and fix the stove. I've been chosen to be that someone. Can you come with me?"

My mouth opened, but the words wouldn't come. My mind raced. Big Bear . . . go up with

Saint in his car. Sit beside Saint like I was really his girl, my hair blowing in the wind. . . . No, I'd have to wear a scarf; otherwise, I'd be a mess. . . .

"Well, what do you say?" He went on. "Jen, are you there?"

I knew I'd say something stupid, and I did. "I'll have to ask my grandmother. I don't want to bother my mother at work—"

"Well, then, ask her." His voice sounded a little impatient.

"Wait a minute," I said weakly. I put the phone down on the bed, started for the door, but then came back again. "When shall I say we'll be back—I mean she's going to want to know." He probably thinks I'm a baby asking for permission, I grumbled to myself. But I knew my grandmother wouldn't let me out without knowing that information.

Saint laughed graciously. "Tell your grandmother we'll be back before dark. The trip up takes only about an hour and forty-five minutes. The gas company wants us up there by one o'clock. They'll do their stuff, and then we can close up. You'll be home by dinnertime, okay?"

"I guess there's no need to ask her then," I said, trying to sound more grown up. "What time do you want to pick me up?"

"About ten o'clock," he said. "Wear something comfortable. We'll want to hike around the area."

I had only one hour! I dashed down the

stairs and found my grandmother in the kitchen.

"That was Saint, wasn't it?" she said. She was making a stuffed chicken for dinner, and she liked to get all the preparations done early in the day.

"Yes," I told her. "And I want to ask you if it's all right if I go up to Big Bear with him for a few hours."

Quickly I told her about the gas man and the St. Clairs' big Thanksgiving reunion coming up. The expression on her face didn't change, and she continued to cut up bread into tiny cubes.

"You should ask your mother," she said, taking the chicken out of the refrigerator.

"But I hate to bother her at work," I told her, scared for a moment that she would come right out and say no.

"You're right," she said, patting her hands on a towel. "Anyway, I believe you're old enough and smart enough to behave yourself, Jen. You have my permission."

I flew to her and hugged her hard. "Oh, Grandma," I said, "thanks! Now I've got to run upstairs and try to make myself look good enough for him."

I could hear my grandmother's, "Humph!" and I knew she thought I looked good enough for anyone, but then she is my grandmother and of course is prejudiced.

I ran smack into Cliff in the dark hallway. He looked tired, and I still felt bad that he was going to have a dull day. To try to cheer him up, I gave him a big smile. But then I would have smiled at King Kong if he'd been there—I was that happy.

"Jenny, I've got a favor to ask," he said.

"Anything," I said generously.

"Can I borrow your typewriter this morning?"

"Sure," I told him. "It's just a little portable," I added as he followed me into my room, "but it does the job."

I hadn't had time to finish the bed, and several jars of stuff were open on the top of my dresser. I'd been sorting through my notebooks for reference material for my career paper, and things were in kind of a mess. I watched his eyes take in the scene. I hoped he wouldn't make a nasty comment about it.

He didn't. He went over to my desk and lifted up the portable, which looked tiny in his big hands. "Thanks," he said smiling. At first I thought he wasn't going to leave. He just stood there, holding the typewriter in his huge hands.

I had to make the first move. Time was flying, and now I had less than an hour. "Well, I've got to hurry," I told him. "Saint just called." Oh, how wonderful the words sounded! "I'm going to go up to Big Bear with him. If you'll excuse me, I've got to get ready."

His expression darkened at the mention of Saint's name, and I had to wonder if he might be jealous. Quickly he backed out of the room, and I shut the door. October in Big Bear would mean warm to hot in the day, cool and then very cool after the sun went down. My pale blue pullover sweater would be perfect, as would the designer jeans my mother bought me over at the Fashion Island. Casual but classy. That's the look I wanted.

I heard the beep of his car, and I ran to my mother's bedroom window and looked out. The bright red of his Porsche Targa gleamed back at me like a jewel in the sun. He was right on time!

We practically flew up the mountain. I'd been up to Big Bear dozens of times with my mother and some kids from school, but I'd never come up in this way. It was as if the car had wings, the tires hardly touching the curving road.

Saint overtook every car, camper, truck, bus, and any other thing moving. He even passed cars where the signs said no passing, and although I knew it was a dangerous thing to do, today it seemed exciting.

He leaned over and pulled the scarf from my head. "But it will blow," I protested. "It'll be a mess by the time we get up there."

"I want to see it free, like we are today, Jen," he said. "Let's just be ourselves for this one day."

It sounded like a wonderful idea to me. I tucked the scarf away in my bag and sat back, letting the cool mountain breezes whip through my hair. He reached over and touched my hand and made it warm with his touch. I had never been so relaxed, so terribly happy. At last I was with Saint, feeling so good, being just myself. He even liked my wild light brown hair.

The music was crazy and wonderful coming out of all sides of his car, as if we were sitting in the middle of a live band and they were playing just for us. A slow song came on then, and he placed his right arm around my shoulders and drew me closer to him. The road got steeper, and the curves melted into more curves. We passed a sign giving us the elevation—6,750 feet. The San Bernardino mountains surrounded us, and the view was fantastic.

"So, your folks are planning a big bash on Thanksgiving?" I asked. "How many people do you think they'll have?" I was talking so casually, so easily.

"Everyone who's important," Saint said, taking the next turn with a squeal of the tires. "Relatives and Dad's important business friends. Maybe some of my friends, too, if I want them."

Maybe Saint will ask me up, I thought wildly, breathing in the pure mountain air. Looking down at the valley, I could see the thick band of yellow that almost always hangs heavily around the Los Angeles, Orange County, and Riverside areas. We had risen above it, just as I had risen above being plain old Jenny Ryan. I was flying high now with Saint, no one could possibly ever ask for more in a date. "Top man," they called him when the subject of football came up. Here I was, little old Jenny Unimportant Ryan, sitting beside him as his special girl!

I could hear him introducing me to his mother at that Thanksgiving bash. "This is the girl who won the scholarship this year. . . ."

"How wonderful," Mrs. St. Clair would say, gasping.

"How very admirable," Mr. St. Clair would say, impressed.

His old grandfather would look at me, thinking, "Now that's the kind of spunky girl I want for my grandson!"

Saint quickly brought me back to reality. "We're almost there," he said, twisting the car onto a private road. He roared the car to a stop in front of an iron gate, hopped out, twisted the lock with his key, swung open the iron gates, and then quickly jumped back into the car. Once inside the gate, he jumped out to lock the gate behind him.

"But how is the gas man going to get in?" I asked. It was so funny, no matter how free and relaxed I felt, still there was that old practical part of me asking stupid questions, interfering with my fun.

"All the utility men have keys to places like this," he said, flashing me his smile. "They have to, in case of emergencies."

"Oh," I said, feeling dumb.

"This iron fence completely surrounds the property," he went on. "True, it's not that high, anyone can climb it, but it helps keep hikers from trespassing, and it gives the place a kind of class."

We were traveling slowly along the dirt road. "I don't want to get my car dirtier than I have to with all that dust," he said as he flicked the switch, closing up our windows. "My father wanted to get the road paved, but my grandfather said it would take away the rustic look of the place."

Huge pines lined both sides of the dirt road. Oleanders everywhere formed hedges well over six feet. Finally we came to a clearing, and there it was: the St. Clair "cabin." A mansion made from logs, if that's possible. There were so many chimneys you couldn't count them fast enough, and a flagstone patio all the way around the house, an outside barbecue made of brick, and an old-fashioned porch swing on one side of the house. I'd never seen anything so impressive, even in magazines.

He parked the car right in front of the patio and unlocked both car doors. Stepping out, I could hear the serene sounds of hundreds of birds chirping. Two squirrels darted between the tall pines, and I jumped. Saint laughed and grabbed for my hand.

"You're going to love it," he said. Who wouldn't, I thought.

From a bunch of keys in his pocket, he finally picked one out and then opened the huge front door. The brown carpeting was so thick it was like walking on clouds. Saint walked over to the massive stone fireplace. He touched a button, and then the drapes slid open. I was standing in the middle of a dream.

All I could say was, "Wow, Saint, it's beautiful!"

He was suddenly by my side. "Not as beautiful as you are, Jen."

He lifted my chin with his two fingers, and it happened. There in that beautiful room, Saint kissed me. But it was nothing like Cliff's kiss. Cliff's kiss had been gentle, as if something was just beginning. Saint's kiss was hard, as if we'd known each other a long time. I didn't like it at all.

But maybe that was Saint's way. Impatient. That's how he drove. Maybe that's how he kissed. Maybe he just didn't know, didn't realize because no one had ever told him, that a kiss should be gentle, with love, warm and sweet.

"Come on, Jen. You're not kissing back. Kiss me back," he said, his voice sounding demanding.

I wanted to kiss him back. I'd dreamed of it for so long that it should have come naturally to me. He took me in his arms, and tilting my head back so that my lips met his, he kissed me again and then again. Each time it was harder, rougher. I gasped for breath.

"Wait," I said. "I can't catch my breath!"

"Then don't," he said. Giving a sharp laugh, he let me go.

My mouth felt bruised. I wanted to wipe off the kiss, but I didn't dare insult him. Instead, I stood there trembling as he walked away from me toward another room.

I followed him like a puppy, feeling foolish. I'd disappointed him. I guessed I would have to learn to kiss like that, and maybe after a while I would learn to like it. Then another thought hit me. Maybe I could teach him to be more gentle. That seemed like a better idea.

"This is our kitchen. Like a restaurant, isn't it?" I walked around him to view it and had to admit he was right. It was massive, a cook's dream. My grandmother would have fainted if she could have seen it.

Then he showed me the bedrooms. Each one had its own fireplace, and the beds were even made up, as if at any moment someone would come through the door to stay the night.

Back in the living room I suddenly wondered how many times Saint had brought Linda up here. I wondered how many times he had kissed her like that and what her reaction had been. With a sickening feeling in the pit of my stomach, I guess I knew. Because she had been Saint's girl for a long, long time.

He pulled me down on the leather sofa in front of the fireplace. His strong arms went around me, and his mouth came down again on mine, and I struggled free.

"Saint, the gas man. He'll be coming any minute now," I said breathlessly. "I don't want him to catch us like this."

I thought Saint would die laughing. It began as a slow rumble and then boomed through the room. He sat straight up on the sofa.

"Gas man!" he said and laughed harder. "You didn't believe that one, did you, Jen? That was for your mother, or in your case, your grandma. I was supplying you with a good story the old folks might go for."

I was on my feet. "What?" I said, not believing him. There's no gas man? You brought me up here for this?"

He pulled me back to the sofa again, but this time I fought him.

"No way!" I shook my head. "You've got the wrong girl, Benjamin St. Clair!"

He tried to grab me, and I could feel my index fingernail cut into the flesh of his right arm as I fought him off. He yelled with the sudden pain.

That same nail that had been broken in June had had plenty of time to grow, and now it had come in handy.

Saint flew to his feet and grabbed at his arm. "You cut me with your lousy nail!"

He ran to the bathroom for some tissue, I guessed, and I darted for the front door. I stood outside, waiting for him. He would get over his anger in a minute and realize his mistake in bringing Jenny Ryan up here. I have to admit I didn't look forward to the ride home. It would be terrible, so different from the ride up. I stood beside the car, not able to get in because it was locked.

I watched him come out of the house, find the key, and then finally turn the lock. He headed straight for the car, not looking at me at all. He climbed in his side, then silently let me in.

The car started with a roar. This time Saint didn't seem to care how much dust he got on his precious Porsche as he sped recklessly toward the gate and then down the mountain.

Soon we came to the little town I'd hardly

noticed on the way up. Saint stopped abruptly in front of what looked like an old general store and, still without a word, got out and went inside the ancient wood-framed building. Somehow I knew it was best for me to stay where I was.

A few minutes later he came out, motioned for me to get out of the Porsche, and handed me a ticket.

"I couldn't deal with having to spend another hour and a half with you. There's a bus leaving at two-thirty," he said coldly. "It'll get you home by dinnertime." Then, before closing his car door, he added, "See ya around."

With that, the car reared into gear and then sped out toward the highway.

I screamed out after him. "Wait, Saint, wait please!" But it was useless. Dejectedly I went inside to wait for the bus.

Chapter 16

The twenty winners of the scholarship competition were set to be posted on the bulletin board in the main entrance hall on Friday morning, October 9. I woke up early that morning, my whole body filled with nervous excitement. Surely I would be one of the twenty. I had worked so hard on my paper.

I met Cliff in the kitchen. In the past few weeks I'd hardly ever bumped into him. He'd been working long hours in the bakery when he wasn't holed up in his room studying. It seemed that the only time I saw him now was in English class. But he sat on the opposite side of the room and except for a few occasional words, hardly ever said anything to me.

It was too early for the rest of the family. He was drinking coffee, and in front of him was a gorgeous, yummy-looking pastry on a napkin.

"Hey, that looks terrific," I said, heading for the refrigerator and a glass of milk.

Quickly he got up and went over to the counter, where he opened a brown paper bag from his bakery.

"I've got another one," he said, pulling it out of the bag.

"No, thank you," I told him, laughing. "If I ate that I'd gain two pounds in fifteen seconds. Thanks, but no thanks!"

It was his turn to laugh now. "Good, you're impressed," he told me, smiling. "What would you say if I told you that this whole thing was only eighty calories?"

"I'd say you were lying," I told him. "I've heard that line before!"

He was serious now. "No, I mean it. This is one of the things I've been working on. Mr. Benny's been helping me for months. We've read all the books on diet cooking and baking, and we've come up with pastries that look good, taste good, but contain only a fraction of the normal calories!"

I looked at him sideways. He didn't seem to be joking.

"Do you know what this means, Jenny?" he went on. "This means that all of those people who have to bypass our bakery because they have weight problems will be able to come in now and enjoy our pastries!"

"You mean it," I said, taking another look at the pastry.

"We really researched this," Cliff said excitedly. "It's going to be a tremendous breakthrough for the baking industry." He walked over to the counter again and from a briefcase pulled out sketches of machines of some kind.

"I've drawn these myself. If we can ever get them actually made, we could save a lot of labor making our fancy diet pastries." He pulled out another page. "What do you think of this floor plan? If we take Mr. Benny's exact floor measurements but rearrange things and add a few new pieces of equipment, we'll have a modern, efficient operation. Mr. Benny will be able to put in fewer hours but still turn out more baked goods than before."

"And those papers?" I asked, as three of them fell on the floor. "The recipes. We've had them tested by two different labs in Los Angeles to assure our customers on the calorie intake and the health value of the ingredients."

I looked at Cliff, who was now breathless. "That's truly amazing. So that's how you've been spending all your time lately."

"You've noticed my absence?" he asked, surprised. Then noticing my blush, he added, "You don't have to answer that." He sat down again and took another swallow of his coffee, while I slid into the chair beside him. "You know, Jenny, when I heard about my dad, I thought I would never be able to be happy again. I was just living for the day he would send for me."

"I know," I whispered. "And I'm still sorry about how you found out."

"But I had to find out," he said, looking down at the pastry in front of him. "I guess we all have to let go of our parents sometime. I just had to let go of my father sooner than most

135

people. Look at you, Jenny. I've actually had more time than you. You lost your father at such a young age, you never even got to know him."

Yes, Cliff, I thought, but I never got to love him either. It was easier for me. If you don't have something to begin with, you can't suffer its loss. But I didn't say it out loud.

I took a bite of the pastry he had placed in front of me. It was filled with some kind of wonderful cheese mixed with apricots.

"Divine!" I told him. "And you're sure it's only eighty calories?"

"The carbohydrate count is low, too," he said. "That's just as important as the calories."

We finished our pastries, and then he looked down at his watch. "I've got to run. Oh, one thing I wanted to ask, and I never seem to get the time. That date you had with the big man, Saint, how was it? I got home so late that night, and your light was already off—"

I took a last quick swallow of milk. "I made it home all right," I told him, not lying. Actually, by the time the bus made it into Sandcastle, I had been one hour late for dinner, but my mother and Mrs. Morrow had stayed over late at the office working with the lawyers on a case due in court the next day, so it had just been my grandmother and me for dinner. I'd told her that we were having such a good time that we lost all track of time. I knew my grandmother knew I was lying. Someday I would tell her, after the pain of the day had gone away.

"Then, are you dating him—exclusively, I mean?"

I tried to laugh, but it was so fake it embarrassed me. "No, Cliff. Saint isn't for me. People like him live in the fast lane. I could never catch up to him, and he has no intentions of slowing down for me."

A funny smile spread over Cliff's face as he picked up his case of papers and cleared the crumbs from the table where he had been eating. He opened the screen door and then looked back at me.

"The guy's a fool," he said, and he was gone, the screen door banging behind him.

There was a huge crowd in front of the bulletin board by the time I got to school. I could hear squeals and screams coming from the kids who'd made it to the front and had found their names on the "lucky twenty" list. Quickly I spotted Tina, who was being shoved so far over to the side she would never make it to the board.

I held my breath when I finally shoved close enough to read the list. It was in alphabetical order, and my eyes slid quickly down the last names until I finally made it to the R's—and there I was! RYAN, Jennifer C. I let out a scream of my own. Hillary Bentwood grabbed me and gave me a bear hug.

"Congratulations," she squealed.

After I got over the first shock of being on the list, I started to read over the other names that would be my competition. Starting at the top in the A's, I worked my way down to the M's and my hand flew to my mouth. MORGAN, Christina M.

I spun around and saw her still behind in the crowd. "Tina, Tina!" I cried out. "You made it!"

She began to cry. Someone grabbed her and gave her a hug, too. The juniors were going crazy with excitement. Then I turned back to the list, my hand sliding down the names. There right under Tina's, as big as life, was MORROW, Clifford R.!

I turned around and searched the crowd. At first I didn't see him, but then there he was, pushing through, and finally he was standing beside me.

"Someone told me, but I had to see for myself," he said, his face all smiles. His hand reached out for mine, and he squeezed it hard. "You made it, too, Jen. But then I knew you would. You worked so hard on your paper. I could hear you typing in there for so many nights. Some of the papers you threw away in the trash—I unfolded them and read them. They were terrific!"

I could feel the blood rushing to my face. "Now I know why you borrowed my typewriter," I told him. "Oh, Cliff, you're going to have yours on the bakery, your pastries."

"It's going to be really great, Jen. Just you wait and see!"

The first class bell rang, and the crowd began to break up, though everyone was still laughing and jabbering to each other. There were only twenty kids on the list, but there must have been fifty well-wishers there, too.

I waved goodbye to Cliff, and I watched Tina, her face still streaked with tears, coming over toward me. Would this ruin it now for Cliff and me? We were beginning to be comfortable with each other—would this competition drive us apart again?

Chapter 17

We had two weeks to put our booths together. Each booth was assigned four students from shop (most of them seniors) to build the framework and necessary counters and display shelves. The design for the inside of the booth had to be strictly up to the booth owner, so all the interiors would be different.

I needed a lot of room for posters. My homemade cosmetic recipes had to be placed where anyone could read them and copy them down. I also had to have a place where I could stack pamphlets showing chemists at work and showing what they had contributed to the cosmetics industry.

Then I had to have a stool where my model would sit while I demonstrated my facials. There would be a small counter where I would mix up homemade cosmetics for the crowd, where I could point out the properties of skin, how chemicals play a great part in keeping it young, and how anyone can experiment with foods found in the home. All of this in one booth—not to mention my display on hair and hands and nails and eye makeup, as well as exercise and diet.

My sign across the top of the booth would read: THE RYAN RITUAL—AND WHAT IT CAN DO FOR YOU! When not busy with the facials, Joann was going to stand in front and hand out circulars with the Ryan Ritual Program, a clear-cut schedule using homemade preparations. Followed faithfully, in only one month's time it was guaranteed to improve one's whole body. It had taken me almost a year to get it all together and over a week to type it. The school office had run the copies off for free because I was one of the twenty winners.

The gym was a mess with amateur carpenters pounding nails and gluing pieces, dropping boards, arguing. There was confusion everywhere, but mostly everyone worked good-naturedly as the excitement of the upcoming competiton mounted.

A couple of students had dropped by to play basketball—I can't imagine where they'd been when the principal's announcement had come over the loudspeaker. They moaned when they saw the activity, and we pushed them back out the door, repeating the principal's message.

The twenty of us had been excused from three days of classes to prepare the booths, and although that seemed like a lot of time in the beginning, we all soon realized that most of us were far from ready.

The gym was to be opened to us until eight-thirty all three nights. I could take advantage of this, but Cliff couldn't, so he had to get in all of his work on his booth during the daytime hours, stopping only long enough to grab a sandwich for lunch.

On the evening of the twenty-first, the second night the gym was open to us, the doors swung open, and a girl stepped through. Another kid so curious she couldn't wait until the big day, I thought wearily.

I was lining up my jars at the time, making sure they matched the little signs over them that explained what they were.

The girl came directly to my booth, without even looking at the others. She had to be a freshman—she looked so "fresh," as if she were right out of a package. Her wispy side-swept blond bangs danced easily over her forehead, and being me, I noticed her skin. The delicate, almost not-there blush on her cheeks made me wonder if she was an expert at applying blush or if it was natural.

"You're Jenny Ryan, aren't you?" she asked, her voice shaking a little.

"Yes," I said. "Can I help you with something?"

"Tina Morgan knows my brother. You know Ted Spring, too, don't you?"

"Oh, yes," I said. "He's new, someone mentioned his name in English the other day."

She gave me a smile. "My brother was telling me about how Tina felt bad that she couldn't help you with your booth because she was going to have a booth of her own. I was wondering if I could maybe be her replacement?"

"But I hadn't thought of replacing her," I told the girl. I knew it would be hard to find another girl who would be willing to sit in front of hundreds of people with all that goo on her for the oily skin demonstration.

"I'll do it," the girl said, flashing me that smile again. "I'd love to."

"Thanks," I said, my mind racing. "But do you know what you're getting into?"

"It's just that I want to be part of something," she explained. And then she extended her hand. "My name's Kathryn Spring, but everyone calls me Katy. I'm new around here and feel kind of lost. My dad told me to stop moaning and groaning about it and get out and involved with something. So here I am."

"The facial is for oily skin," I warned her.

"That's okay," she said. "I have oily skin."

I bet, I thought. She had perfect skin, but I knew the facial wouldn't hurt her no matter what kind of skin she had. We were only going to go through it twice anyway.

"Fine, then," I said smiling. "We don't really need to practice it, but you'll need to be here at five-thirty. The doors open at six. Just so you know, people will be wandering in and out of here constantly from six until eight. The judges will give the final decision around eight-thirty.

And bring a towel for your shoulders and a band to keep your hair back, okay? I'll bring the tissues and everything else we'll need."

She put up her hand in a gesture to show that she understood the arrangement. "I'll be here on time," she said excitedly before running out the gym doors.

Tina was sitting on the floor, putting the final touches on her booth when I walked over to her. She and her mother had spent many nights sewing the blue and white organdy curtains to completely cover her booth, the colors matching the outside of the Victorian dollhouse. The house was to be the main attraction in the booth, and Tina's pamphlets told of wallpaper hints and decorating schemes for anyone interested in interior decorating. She had wallpapered each little room in that fabulous house, and the tiny furniture her uncle had made for her was placed with a great deal of care. Tina wanted to do a lot of serious studying in Europe and New York if she won, something she'd probably not be able to do without a scholarship of some kind.

I had to admit she'd done a beautiful job with her booth. I would have never guessed she had it in her. But the biggest surprise for me was Tina's mother, who must have come home from her night shift and worked all the way into morning to help her sew all those curtain panels. I'd always thought that her mother was a little uninterested in anything Tina did. I had never heard her say anything to her daughter except in a gruff, commanding way. But looking at Tina's booth again, I thought of her differently. Tina's mother loved her as much as my mother loved me. She just showed it in a different way.

Tina and I were done, and with only half an hour left until the custodian would come and close the gym, we decided to walk around and look at the other booths. Number one had been assigned to Doreen Hanson, who wanted to be a veterinarian.

John Mendoza had booth number two, and because he wanted to be a mechanic, his whole area was filled with machines he would use for his demonstrations.

Number three belonged to Bob Bailey and his display of landscaping and gardening. Next came Tina's with her interior decorating. Oil paintings decorated booth number five, owned by Ruth Pritcher, and number six, Mark Andrews, displayed pictures of an architect at work.

At number seven, Ted Ricker showed us why biology would be a good career for him, and number eight was filled with pictures and pamphlets of dancing, because Marian Temper had her heart set on being a dancing teacher.

Suzanne Crate displayed everything a dietician needed to know at booth number nine, and Phillip Lehmann told us why he wanted to be a language teacher at booth number ten.

Booth number eleven was fantastic, but

then maybe I was just a little prejudiced. Cliff had done a wonderful job on his bakery display. Mr. Benny's borrowed pastry machine took up most of the booth, but a visit to this area would be really worthwhile and delicious at the same time. Cliff planned to stand behind the counter making his diet pastries, backed up by all kinds of posters of chefs and bakers working in Italy, France, and all parts of Europe. Mr. Benny had collected the posters himself from attending baking conferences in those countries, and he said he'd never had a reason before to unroll them.

I had a pretty good idea that Mr. Benny really liked Cliff, and from all the conversation I picked up between Mrs. Morrow and her son, I had the idea that Mr. Benny, a bachelor, was teaching Cliff the trade like he would have taught his own son if he had ever had one.

Randy Templeton had the booth right next to Cliff's. He wanted to be a boat builder, and his booth was so professionally done that I began to get concerned about my competition.

Booth thirteen held a small black spinet on which Lydia Grace would demonstrate why she would make a great piano teacher. At booth fourteen Tom Hernandez displayed his photography, while at fifteen Patricia Kendall had dangled a skeleton. She wanted more than anything to be a doctor.

A display by Melanie Bowers on travel agencies was next to her. There I was, at booth seventeen, and I had to admit I loved my signs and all the lights in the gym hitting my colored jars.

Bob Reynolds was right next to mine. He wanted to make furniture like his father, and his displays were fantastic.

Larry Schneider would probably be a great prosecuting attorney someday; his booth, number nineteen, was full of law enforcement information. A police officer from Sandcastle was also going to put in an appearance and answer any questions the public asked.

The last booth, number twenty, was owned by Mary Jane Fiddler, and it was stacked full of computers she'd got on loan from her father's company. She would give a great demonstration on the latest thing in that line.

As I turned to look at them, I realized for the very first time that I had some stiff competition. And for the very first time I began to worry.

The custodian, Mr. Hooper, came in and waved at the students still working on their displays. "There's always tomorrow," he said, laughing. "Anyhow, they all look done to me. I've never seen such good-looking booths."

He probably said that every year, but then I remembered I had heard someone else say the same thing. Maybe we *were* extra good this year. Everywhere kids were getting ready to leave.

"Let's get on home," Tina said. I took one more look at the great displays and followed her out the door. A shadow stepped out of the darkness, and Saint loomed up in front of me. Tina immediately backed away.

"Wait, Tina," I called out to her. "Don't leave without me."

She stood still in the background as I had asked, while Saint moved closer to me. His eyes searched mine seriously. Although I wanted nothing more to do with him, I had to admit he looked almost irresistible in his green shirt and tight jeans. He ground out a cigarette with his cowboy boot and then gave me his full attention.

"Jen, I can't tell you how sorry I am about leaving you up there."

I put up my hand to stop him. "No problem, Saint," I said calmly. "The bus ride was long, but it got me home. There's no need for you to feel bad. It all worked out fine." My heart wasn't even beating rapidly, the way it always had when I talked to him before.

I turned to Tina, who was still standing there, her eyes big, wondering what would happen next. "Come on, Tina, I've got to get home now."

"I'll drive you, I'll drive you both if you want," Saint said.

I smiled my very best smile. "Thank you, Saint, but no thanks. Tina and I need the exercise." I gave Tina a look, and she caught it, and the two of us started walking away from the gym.

"Don't look back," I told Tina. "Look straight ahead. He'll stand there for a moment, thinking maybe I'll change my mind, but when he finally figures out that I won't, he'll get in his gorgeous car across the street and rev up that motor just to show us he has power. Then he'll speed by us so fast it will cause a breeze and leave us here to taste the dust."

We had walked about one block before the car tore by us. I could taste the leftover dust.

"You know him pretty well, don't you, Jenny?" Tina said.

"Pretty well," I told my friend. "Pretty well."

Chapter 18

It was six o'clock in the morning when my mother received that terrible phone call. She ran directly into my bedroom, in the process waking up the whole household.

"Jenny," she yelled, "Jenny, an awful thing happened!"

I grabbed my robe, threw it around me, and darted out of bed. Behind my mother stood my grandmother, and right behind her were Mrs. Morrow and Cliff, who was trying to wipe the sleep out of his eyes.

"The school called," my mother said, her voice shaking. "Mr. Hooper, the custodian, arrived there about five-thirty, and Jen—" There were tears in her eyes. Had someone died?

"What is it?" I asked, trembling.

"Some people across the street from the school said that a gang of boys was making a lot of noise in front of the school last night. The gang left and—well, they must have broken into the school—"

"The displays—the booths," Cliff interrupted, his eyes full of fear. "Did they get to the gym?"

My mother started to cry. "The one whole side, booths fourteen through twenty. They wrecked them all."

Seventeen! That would mean mine!

"Oh, no!" I cried out. "I don't believe it!"

I scrambled around in my closet, grabbing the first clothes I could find, my jeans and a sweater. I was blubbering something about getting down there. My grandmother started to cry, and Mrs. Morrow put her arm around me.

"I'll drive you down there, Jenny. Maybe we can all work together. We've got this whole day and night."

"When the office opens, I'll call in for both of us," my mother said. "I'll tell them it's an emergency."

Cliff came over to me. "Maybe it won't be so bad. We'll just all go down and take a look, and then we'll know what to do."

Everyone went to their rooms to get dressed. Then we all drove down in Mrs. Morrow's old Ford. No one said a word. There was really nothing to talk about until we could see the actual damage.

Three police cars were parked in front of the school. The gym doors were open, and there were about thirty people standing around them, none of them smiling.

A photographer from our newspaper was putting film into his camera, a lady was interviewing our principal out on the sidewalk. Mr. Baxter was trying to answer her questions and listen to someone else talk right beside him. Mr. Baxter shook his head and took quick puffs from his cigarette. His hair, for the first time, was uncombed. I looked down at his feet and saw bedroom slippers.

I moved like a robot through the crowd. Cliff at one point reached out and caught my hand and pulled me along like a lost child. When I entered the gym, I wanted to cover my eyes. I saw Patricia Kendall over in one corner of the gym, tears streaming down her face. Her skeleton has been torn apart, its bones all over the gym floor. Her booth had been stripped down to the wood.

My grandmother gasped, and I followed her eyes. My beautiful booth was a mess! A horrible mess of creams, of jars spilled over, smashed glass everywhere. The creams had been viciously smeared over everything. My signs had been torn down, defaced with black and red crayons and spray paint. The artificial daisies that bordered the booth had been smashed and pulled out of their wires. If it hadn't been for Cliff's strong arm, I would have crumbled to the floor.

Mr. Hooper ran over to us and gave us several boxes. "You might want to use these to clean up," he said. He looked so sad, I thought he was going to cry at any moment.

"The vandals!" my grandmother said, scowling.

"How could they!"

"It's the only way some kids can get attention," Cliff said.

"I hope they catch them," my grandmother added.

"It wouldn't matter to most of them," Cliff said bitterly, starting to pile some of my broken jars into one of the boxes. "Then they would get the attention they wanted."

"I know what you mean," my mother said, picking up a few of my ruined posters. "I hear of cases all the time where the kids who can't make it any other way do something vicious like this."

I knew they were both right, but it didn't help to soothe my hurt feelings or put my booth back together again. It was all over for me now.

We were all crowded around our ruined displays when Mr. Baxter entered the gym.

"I want to express my deep sorrow over this terrible event," he told us. "The school will, of course, pay for all damages. However, the main thing is that none of you students will lose out on your opportunity to participate in this function. The staff of Sandcastle High will assist all of you in reconstructing your booths in time for the competition."

I could see the perspiration forming on his forehead. He took a handkerchief out of his pocket and wiped it off.

"We wish we could postpone the whole program for another day or so, but unfortunately four of the six judges are coming from out of town and can't stay longer. I wish you all good luck, and remember we'll be here to assist you in any way we can. The gym, of course, will stay open all day, and Chief Powers has assured us that he will supply us with his men to stand guard throughout the night. Thank you."

"We'll do it!" Cliff said.

"Do what?" I asked, licking the tears from my mouth.

"We'll reconstruct. We'll make it as good as new."

I began to laugh hysterically. Maybe I was going crazy. My mother looked at me anxiously.

"Impossible!" I shouted at him above the noise of the crowd. "Absolutely impossible!" I'd have to make all those mixtures again. Those soaps! The daisies—we'd have to buy hundreds of daisies again. Everything would have to be rebuilt. You're crazy, Cliff. It can't be done."

"Oh, yes, it can," Cliff said. "All of us together. Your grandmother can mix up those soaps. You can give me some of your recipes, and I can help. I'm good at following recipes, you know. Your carpenters are going to rebuild the booth itself. My mother is very good at typing. She'll redo anything that's been destroyed—and I can print your signs better than you did."

He seemed to have everything figured out. I shook my head and started to cry again, and then I looked over at the other students who had lost their booths. All of their parents were hanging around them, too, and their friends were all talking about how they would rebuild.

Some of the students were crying, but then

I could see they were slowly being caught up in the enthusiasm of their family and friends. By now the other owners of the untouched booths had been notified, and they had arrived and were all talking about how they would help out with the damaged ones.

Tina came over to me and put her arm around my shoulders. "I'll do anything to help you get it back together again."

It was going to be okay. It would take all day and most of the night, but we were all going to make it.

Most of my repairs could be done at home with my whole family working into the night. Cliff took over the kitchen, my recipes spread out in front of him. My grandmother unpacked the soaps she had made for Christmas presents—she'd have plenty of time to make more, she told me. My mother drove down to the stores and hunted up some more artificial daisies, and Mrs. Morrow typed madly from my original material for my pamphlets. Luckily I had kept all my original drafts at home. I was glad that I never threw anything away! When Mrs. Morrow finished, she headed for the school to make the copies.

Cliff was right. He *did* print better than I did, and my signs looked great as I helped my crew of carpenters tack them onto the top of my booth.

The whole gym hummed with activity. We'd show those creeps they couldn't ruin our booths. In fact, because of all the wonderful help, most of the destroyed booths looked better than they had before. Some of the local business people, hearing the news, donated supplies and equipment to a few of the kids who couldn't otherwise recreate their displays on such short notice. One doctor, for instance, offered Patricia Kendall a skeleton plus colored posters of vertebrae that she hadn't had before and all kinds of important-looking pamphlets. It was so fantastic to see how things could be worked out.

"There's a warm feeling around my heart when I see people turn a bad thing into a good one," my grandmother said at the dinner table that night. We stopped just long enough to eat before leaving for the gym to set up all of my new creams and cosmetics and signs. Cliff and I would put the finishing touches to my booth and then walk home together.

I finished my grandmother's baked ham, green beans, and sweet potatoes and thanked her again for letting me use her soaps. In all of the rush of the day, she had found the time to see that we were all properly nourished. Cliff passed me the tray of ham again, and I caught his smile. I had a warm feeling around my heart, too. I never could have gotten through this mess without him.

We left the gym around ten-thirty that night. Mr. Benny had given Cliff the night off, which was a very generous thing to do, since Cliff was going to have to be off the following night, too. All the booths were in perfect order again, and this time there would be a police officer standing watch inside the gym all night. So, we didn't have anything to worry about.

The stars sparkled like jewels in the October night, and Cliff grabbed my hand as we walked toward home.

"The big day is almost here," Cliff said.

"Cliff, I can't begin to thank you for helping me like that," I told him. "I could have never done it alone—in fact, I don't think I would have tried."

"Some things you can't do alone," Cliff told me. "And don't think I helped you because I felt sorry for you, Jenny."

We were under a huge tree in front of Mr. Brown's old Victorian house. It looked almost like Tina's model. He stopped me right under that tree, and then I was leaning back against the trunk of that old tree, and Cliff was kissing me gently.

"I helped you because I love you, Jenny Ryan," he said, and he kissed me again and again until I found it hard to catch my breath. But it wasn't like the time with Saint. There was nothing scary about this; there was only warmth and tenderness. I kissed Cliff back, and he didn't have to ask me.

"If I win, you'll hate me," I whispered between his kisses.

He laughed. "No, I won't, Jenny. But if I win, will you hate me?"

It was my turn to laugh. "Impossible," I told him. And then I turned quickly and started to run, knowing full well he would soon catch up to me.

"But you'd better get used to the idea of me winning!" I shouted back at him, laughing all the while. "Because I'm going to!"

Chapter 19

October 23.

Slowly I opened my eyes to the familiar sounds of the waves crashing on the rocks. No pitter-patter of rain like it does once in a while in our area of the world in October. The sun would rain down its brilliance on my day, and when it finally set, it would be time for the competition.

The final moment tonight, when the principal would tear open the judges' sealed envelope, would be mine as well. Sitting on my bed, I could almost hear it now, over the roar of the waves, as though the waves were applauding me. "And the winner is—Jenny Ryan!"

I will cry, of course, I thought. Don't winners always get a little teary? And my picture would be in the local paper. Maybe even the *Los Angeles Times* would pick it up, too. They did that sometimes. And my mother and grandmother would be so proud of me.

I'd have to choose my college quickly now that I knew the money would be there. Without wasting any more time, I hopped out of bed and started getting out the clothes I would wear to school. Even though I was one of the twenty finalists, I still had to attend regular classes today.

Five o'clock.

It was the first time I'd ever worn my turquoise velour dress, and when I looked at myself in the closet mirror, I was pleased. My bone-colored shoes matched the smock I would wear over the dress. My grandmother had made it especially for the occasion, and she had even embroidered my name on the pocket.

"It'll make you look like a professional chemist, working right in the lab," she told me.

I kissed her goodbye. Mrs. Morrow and my mother were not home yet. They had planned to dash home about five-fifteen, pick up grandma, and head for the school, where they would eat hot dogs and ice cream out on the football field with all the other parents and friends of the exhibitors.

My grandmother sat very still when I kissed her cheek, and then she turned and kissed mine. "Jen," she said, "in case you don't win—"

"But I'm going to win, Grandma." I laughed.

"That's a good way to feel, honey," she said, smiling. "But just in case you don't. In my heart, you're still the winner."

I kissed her again and flew out the door.

Five-thirty.

Joann and Katy were there as they had both promised. Joann wore a powder blue dress, the nice open neckline making her long, lovely neck look even longer. Perfect for the demonstration.

Katy looked great, too. She wore a neat little brown pantsuit, and when she took off the jacket, I noticed that the gold blouse underneath brought out the gold in her hair.

The gym doors were still locked, but somehow or other a few students had drifted in. A girl about Katy's age came up to my booth while I was rearranging my jars. Her face was covered with freckles.

"Jenny Ryan?" she asked meekly.

"Yes," I told her impatiently. "I'm sorry, but the booth isn't open yet. They said six—"

"Oh, but I've got to talk to you," she went on breathlessly. "Later on you might be too busy, and I've got to have some information!"

I looked at her face, so full of concern. "What's wrong?" I asked, putting the jars down.

"It's my freckles," she said. "I heard you have a fabulous formula to make them disappear."

I started to laugh, looked across the gym, and saw Cliff working in his booth. He smiled and waved. He'd gone directly from school to the bakery, and Mr. Benny had said he'd help him get the pastries to the booth. And then I turned back to the girl in front of me.

"My name is Robin Adrian. I don't even go to school here yet. I'm still over at George Washington, but I'll be here next year."

I took another look at Robin. She reminded

me of a girl named Jenny Ryan way back in the painful eighth grade. I had to help her.

"Okay, Robin," I said. "But then you've got to run outside and wait until the doors officially open."

I had put a pad of paper and a jar filled with pencils on the counter for my customers. "Here, write this down," I told her, reciting the recipe I knew so well.

She smiled. "Oh, thank you, Jenny Ryan. No matter who wins, you're the winner with me!" She turned and ran out the gym doors.

Five minutes before six.

The gym was starting to hum with activity. There wasn't anything else left to do at my booth, so I decided to rush over to Tina's and wish her luck for the umpteenth time.

"It's beautiful," I told her.

She smiled. "Thank you, Jenny. Yours is beautiful, too. In fact, I'd say we have a lot of competition in here."

"That's for sure," I answered.

"You know, Jen," Tina said, "winning tonight would be making a dream come true for my mother. When we're together, sometimes she tells me how she wished things could have been different for her, for both of us. So you see, Jenny, if I won she'd be winning, too."

I looked around the room. "It's a shame we can't all win," I said sincerely, looking at all of the faces I knew so well by now.

I looked over at Cliff's booth. He wanted to win, too, just as much as I did. It would guarantee him a good career, studying with the finest bakers in the world, learning new techniques, maybe getting his sketches of machinery actually made into the real thing. Again our eyes met, and we both smiled shyly. Falling in love was a funny feeling. Really falling in love, that is. The feeling I'd had for Saint was nothing like what I felt about Cliff. This was real. It had taken awhile. We had had some bumpy times, sometimes I even thought I hated him, but then it had all gradually come together, and I knew it was real now.

I said goodbye to Tina as six o'clock approached. The twenty of us were at our booths as the gym doors swung open.

The roar of the crowd reached to the high rafters of the gym—laughing, talking, asking questions, and calling to friends: "Over here. Come over here and see this!" It was like one big swap meet—rows and rows of people shoving past, some stopping, some pressing on to other areas.

I'd decided to do Joann first. She sat on the stool, the towel around her neck, a band keeping her hair away from the mixture. I told the gathering crowd all about the benefits of the dry skin facial and told them also that in fifteen minutes or so I would be giving another one for oily skin. Katy stood at the back of the booth, happy to be involved in it all.

Some people clapped when I gave Joann the final rinse and showed them how her face glowed. Some even hung around waiting for my next demonstration. When I finally pulled Katy to the stool, the people around my booth were entranced.

Some of them were eating pastries and had pamphlets clutched in their hands. Others had come prepared with shopping bags. These were mostly the people who came every year and knew just how things would be.

I could hear the oohing and ahhing at some of the booths. Sometimes I could hear the tinkle of Lydia's piano through the din. People loved that. She was really good, and her playing entertained the crowd as they passed by.

Once in a while a police officer's voice boomed over it all, and I could hear the constant hum of Mary Jane's computers in her demonstrations.

Joann and Katy spent most of their time between demonstrations handing out my literature and recipes for homemade cosmetics. I could hear people say to each other, "Hey, look what you can do with avocados!"

Once I saw Robin Adrian in the crowd. She waved and smiled, and I knew she would be using my freckle remover as soon as she could whip it up.

Finally it was eight-thirty. The crowd sensed the frayed nerves of the competitors. I stood on a box in the back of my booth and looked over the gym. Cliff was looking my way. He sensed my terrible nervousness, I guessed, but then he, too, had so much at stake now.

The judges would be announcing the winner in just moments. Cliff's eyes met mine and held, as if there were not a whole gym full of people between us. Then he raised his hand and clear across the gym floor, he blew me a kiss. Strangely enough, I could feel it land on my lips. I touched my mouth—it was almost as if he had come over and kissed me.

It was then, as I looked down at all of my jars of creams and my posters, pamphlets, soaps, and recipes, that the strangest thing happened to me.

Mr. Baxter had just carried a wooden box up to the front of the gym where the stage ordinarily would be. Someone was now helping him step up on it. He held a piece of paper in his hand and then cleared his throat. In his other hand was a microphone with a long, dangling wire, which he whipped around him, cautioning people not to fall over it. In seconds the crowd had stopped yelling, the talk had stopped, the laughter had stilled. Twenty of us—and only one name would be called.

"I first want to thank all of you. This has been the very finest year, the finest career day I have ever seen. Even when we had trouble with the terrible maliciousness that occurred here, we all pulled through beautifully, thanks to our business and professional people in our town of Sandcastle."

The people gave out a roar of approval and clapped their hands. Mr. Baxter put up his hand for silence again.

"I also want to thank our six fine judges, who have so generously given their time. Their job was a tough one, almost an impossible one, but it has been done. Now I want to announce the winner."

The crowd was still again. Joann's face was so white I wanted to ask her if she was okay, but I didn't want to miss the announcement. I knew Katy was holding her breath.

But what was happening to me? I had wanted to win so badly. But now the strangest thing was happening. I wanted to hear Mr. Baxter call out Cliff's name more than anything in the world.

There was dead silence as the principal sliced open the envelope. The piece of paper made a crinkling sound as he unfolded it and held it up to the light. Then his voice shook as he called out, "Miss Christina M. Morgan—interior decorating!"

A hush that lasted only a split second was followed then by thunderous applause. I could hear shouts of, "Tina! Tina!" as the whole world was swimming around me, going mad.

I was so happy for my friend I didn't have time to register disappointment at losing. Tina would get her dream after all. Joann and I abandoned my booth, and squeezed through the throng beginning to surround Tina. I had just enough time to hug her before she was overcome by the flash of cameras and the judges and other school people waiting for her. We'd have time for our own private celebration later, I concluded, turning away from the approaching crowd. This was Tina's moment to shine.

It was after I moved away from Tina's booth that the disappointment set in. I had lost, and Cliff had lost, and suddenly I felt the urgent need to get out of that room and sort out my thoughts.

I don't know just how I made my way out of the gym, but I did. Without stopping I headed toward home, the crisp night air flying by me. I knew if I stopped for one second, I would start crying, and I didn't want to. That would be so babyish—and I was beyond that, I thought. Still, my head was so mixed up. Here I wanted to win so badly all along, but then in the last few minutes I'd wanted more than anything to have Cliff win. What was going on?

I crossed the street that went by the front of my house, and a few seconds later I reached the beach. My body was exhausted as I flung myself down into the sand. In those last few minutes I had wanted Cliff to win so much. My disappointment was so great that I held my head, and the tears just spilled out all over the place. I knew my mascara was running because some of it got in my eyes, and for a moment I had a painful time trying to get it out with a tissue from my pocket. The tissue got so wet that I had to throw it away. But still the tears came.

Someone touched my shoulder, and I jumped and turned. It was Cliff. I dissolved in his arms, blubbering about how I was so disappointed. I was sure he couldn't make out my words because they were so mixed up with my sobbing.

"I'm sorry you didn't win, too," he said softly, pushing my tangled hair away from my face, kissing me on my trembling mouth. "You know, Jen, it was the strangest thing. I had knocked myself out for so long wanting to win, and then in those last few moments—remember when I threw you a kiss? Well, from that moment on, I wanted to hear them call out your name. So you see, I must love you that much."

I stopped crying now. "But it was the same for me," I told him. "I wanted *you* to win."

He started to laugh. "Your mascara's running again. Really, Jen, you should try to develop something that will be waterproof if you intend to go through life crying at the slightest little disappointment."

"This wasn't slightest. We lost, Cliff Morrow! That's a cold fact. We lost!"

"Did we?" Cliff pulled me to my feet. "Come on, let's walk a little."

I pulled off my shoes. They were so filled with sand I felt I was walking with weights strapped to my feet.

"Are you sorry Tina won?" he asked.

"Of course not. I mean, if I couldn't win and you couldn't, I'm glad it went to her."

"So why are you crying?" he asked again. "Be happy for her."

I looked at him and smiled. "Sometimes you're too logical for your own good," I said. The tears had begun to stop.

"We'll just have to work a little harder for what we want, Jenny," he said, pulling me by the hand. "I figure if we both wanted each other to win, then that must be a good sign. If we can just keep that same feeling for each other the rest of our lives, we'll make it."

He stopped and pulled me into his arms. "What do you say you go with me to the Halloween party next week?" he asked, his eyes warm and suddenly happy.

"I'd love to," I told him. But how could he think of a Halloween party now?

"I want you to go as a clown. In fact, we'll both go as clowns." He kissed me firmly, as if he were planting a kiss that would stay forever. "I happen to love clowns," he added.

We walked some more, his hand pulling me along, as it probably would for the rest of our lives. But I figure he was right. We hadn't lost a thing. In fact, I think we both had won something more precious than anything else in the world.